Growing Up Adopted

MAXINE B. ROSENBERG

Growing Up Adopted

Afterword by Lois Ruskai Melina,
author of *Raising Adopted Children*

BRADBURY PRESS   NEW YORK

Bradbury Press
An Affiliate of Macmillan, Inc.
866 Third Avenue, New York, NY 10022
Collier Macmillan Canada, Inc.
Printed and bound in the United States of America
First Edition
10 9 8 7 6 5 4 3 2 1

The text of this book is set in 12 point Baskerville.
Book design by Julie Quan

LIBRARY OF CONGRESS CATALOGING-IN-PUBLICATION DATA
Rosenberg, Maxine B.
Growing up adopted / by Maxine B. Rosenberg.
p. cm.
Bibliography: p.
Includes index.
Summary: Fourteen adoptees of various ages describe
their experiences and feelings about being adopted
and their relationships with their adopted
and, in some cases, their birth families.
ISBN 0-02-777912-2
1. Children, Adopted—United States—Psychology—Case studies—
Juvenile literature. 2. Adoptees—United States—Psychology—
Case studies—Juvenile literature. 3. Interracial
adoption—United States—Case studies—Juvenile literature.
4. Intercountry adoption—United States—Case studies—
Juvenile literature.
[1. Adoption.] I. Title.
HV875.55.R67   1989
362.7'34'0973—dc20   89-9899 CIP AC

ACKNOWLEDGMENTS

My sincere thanks to the people and organizations who made this book possible: Family Resources, Ossining, New York, for their time and involvement and for trusting me with their children; Betty Klee for leading me to the right sources; Debbie Wenninger who in many ways contributed to this project; Joe Soll of Adoption Circle, for always finding the time; the adults and children who shared their lives with me and taught me so much; Sharon Steinhoff, my editor, who always manages to see the light at the end of the tunnel; my sons, Mark, David, and Seth, and my daughter, Karin, for being great kids; my husband, Paul, my best friend and best fan; and most of all to Welcome House Adoption Agency for bringing me my daughter, Karin.

With love to Karin—my girl

CONTENTS

GROWING UP ADOPTED

Growing Up Adopted

ON WRITING THIS BOOK

While statistics on adoption are imprecise, it's estimated that there are six million adoptees in the United States—half of them children. Another way to think of this number is, of our total population, one person in fifty is adopted.

As a parent of one of these children, a Korean-born daughter (as well as three biological sons), I have been able to observe firsthand how adoption affects each member of the family—the adopted child, the parents, the siblings (adopted or biological), and the extended family. At the time I wrote *Being Adopted* (Lothrop, Lee & Shepard, 1984), my daughter was eight years old. Most of the issues I described then concerned children my daughter's age. For *Growing Up Adopted,* which explores the feelings of older children as well as adults, I had to delve into other people's lives and experiences,

1

to compare their stories with the "facts" about adoption.

I began by reading the latest publications on adoption. I also spoke with psychologists who have worked with adopted children, social workers at adoption agencies, and numerous adoptive parents.

Nothing I had learned about adoption from my own experience and from this research could, however, compare to what I discovered after interviewing the people who agreed to be part of this book. Sifting through hours and hours of taped interviews in search of themes, patterns, and perhaps hidden truths has been an eye-opening journey. And listening to the stories of the adults and children has made vivid how attitudes toward adoption have changed since the 1960s, and the impact this has had on the adoptee.

In the past, most adoptees were young, healthy, white American children. Because they were somewhat physically similar to their parents, few questioned the circumstances of their birth. This made it easier for parents to delay telling their children about their adoption or not to tell them at all.

Parents were encouraged in this secrecy by lawyers, social workers, and physicians involved in adoption as well as by relatives and friends. Nearly all believed that withholding birth information from adopted children benefited the child. Also, as recently as twenty years ago, our culture did not celebrate differences as it does today. Parents then often felt ashamed or embarrassed if they were not able to give birth and so concealed their child's adoption.

One man I interviewed discovered he was adopted at age thirty-three. Another, a woman, learned the truth of her birth one month before her wedding. Other now-adult adoptees found out the news from neighborhood children or from an overheard family conversation. Unfortunately, these adoptees reacted with anger. They could not understand why their parents would keep the facts about their birth from them. In some instances, adult adoptees were so angry that I could not include them in the book. Those that were retained were kept as a commentary on how times have changed and because their anger has cooled as they've gained perspective on their adoption.

Today a sizable number of adoptees are foreign-born. Their adoptive families are usually of a different race and culture. According to the National Committee for Adoption, Americans adopted over ten thousand babies from abroad in the year 1987 alone. Most of these children were born in Korea and South America, and most of the adoptive parents were Caucasian. The committee reports that more American minority children are being adopted, too.

Since many young adoptees today do not physically blend into their families, the fact of their adoption is a much more accepted part of their lives. Unlike the adults I interviewed, the younger children—whether they were of the same race as their family or not—knew they were adopted as far back as they could remember. Although they might not have understood the meaning of adoption when they were told about it, nevertheless it was a word they were familiar with as they grew up. By the time they were ready to learn more about their birth, they felt comfortable asking their parents to supply them with the information.

Because of their youth and mostly positive adoptive experiences, many of the children I interviewed insisted that adoption was not an important issue in their lives— that it, in fact, hardly affected them at all. In many cases, they found it difficult to detail their feelings on the subject. Instead, they were more eager to tell me about the concerns they had in common with most kids— friends, school, sports. Even so, all had at some time in their lives been forced to think about what constitutes a family, which biological children rarely contemplate. In general, I found their understanding of the concept of family to be quite sophisticated for children their age.

Today in most states and foreign countries, adoption records are sealed by court orders as a way to "protect the child." With some variations, adoption records include the original birth certificate, the name(s) of birth parent(s), adoption agency reports (if an agency is involved), the medical history, and a physical description of the birth parent(s). Now that the secrecy that has surrounded adoption is fading, many adoptees and birth parents are working hard to open these court records so anyone who chooses to search will find the process easier. Three adults who have decided to search for their birth parents are included in *Growing Up Adopted* to show the variety of possible outcomes.

Most of the children I spoke to had already asked their mother or father questions about their birth parents and, at the moment, felt satisfied with what they were told. All of them said that if indeed they did search one day, they were sure their mother and father would help them.

On the other hand, a number of the adult adoptees worried that by searching they would hurt their adoptive parents' feelings. "Mom might think I didn't love her anymore," one said. Another, wanting to protect his elderly parent, said he might consider search after his mother was no longer alive.

By the time the book was completed, I felt a personal attachment to all the individuals who told me their stories. And, so often, that feeling was reciprocated. "You made me soul search," one man said in thanks. "I got to know things about myself I never realized," said another. One child kissed me good-bye. Another walked me to the elevator, holding my hand.

In some cases, subjects asked that their names be changed so they could feel freer to speak frankly—a request I have respected. For the same reason, a few people asked not to be photographed. To protect their privacy and that of the child whose adoption is not finalized, I chose to omit photographs altogether.

In the end, both the subjects and I have grown from this project. They learned things about themselves that in many instances they had not put into words before. And I learned more about what it means to be adopted. I hope others—adoptees young and old, parents, and social service workers—will equally benefit from these candid conversations.

Maxine B. Rosenberg
May 1989

"There are different ways to build families"

JOSH, age 10

When Josh was three months old his parents flew to Colombia, South America, to adopt him. Three years later they returned to that country and brought home his sister, Marisa, who was three-and-a-half months old at the time. Josh still remembers that day. "My aunt and uncle took me to the airport to meet my parents when they came off the plane. Mom was carrying the baby. As soon as she saw me, she asked if I wanted to hold Marisa. I said yes. I was the first one to have my sister in my arms. I'll never forget that."

Then he recounts his own entry into the family. Although Josh usually loves to tease and clown around, now he's very serious. "Mom and Dad were trying to adopt a baby for a long time—two-and-a-half years. One morning they got a phone call from a person at an agency in Colombia. The woman told them about me and said she even had a picture to show them. My parents drove for over an hour just to see that photograph. When they had to go to work the next day, they argued over who would take the picture with them."

Once Josh was home, his parents wanted to celebrate his long-awaited arrival. "Mom says that they invited seventy people to this big party just to meet *me*. Of course I don't remember any of it, but I still like hearing the story."

Josh knows how much his parents had wanted children and how important adopting was for them. November 7 and June 18—the dates Josh and Marisa came into the family—are always celebrated as special days. "Usually the four of us go out for dinner, and the child whose day it is gets to pick the place. When I was younger we went to McDonald's or Burger King. This year I chose a Chinese restaurant."

Sometimes when the family is out together Josh notices people staring at them. While Josh and Marisa have dark brown hair and eyes and tannish skin, their father has red hair, blue eyes, and a fair complexion. "If we're just with Mom it's not so obvious we're adopted. She has rather dark hair and dark eyes too, so strangers must think we look alike. But when we're with Dad, I can tell people wonder if we're adopted. Recently I told Mom that Dad's the person in our family who stands out— *he's* the different one."

Josh says he's glad he has a sister whose coloring resembles his own. "Because Marisa and I are both sort of brownish, and from Colombia, somehow it makes me feel we're the same. I also like having a sister who's adopted, too," Josh admits.

By the time Marisa arrived, Josh already knew a little bit about adoption. "Mom and Dad told me that adoption was another way to have a child. They also explained that I grew inside my first mother's stomach, but she wasn't able to keep me. I remember hearing these things and using the word 'adoption,' but I'm not sure how much I understood."

Once Marisa was a part of the family, Josh became more curious about his beginnings. "I asked my parents if they knew my birth mother's name and age, and they did. But when I asked them to describe my father, there was nothing they could tell me. Now that I'm getting older, I want to learn even more about the subject of adoption, especially my own."

In the future, Josh plans to meet his birth parents. "Mainly I'd like to find out how they're doing and if they're all right. I'm also curious to see if there's a resemblance between them and me. I haven't talked to Mom and Dad about this, but I think they'd help me and be encouraging. Awhile ago I told them I wanted to go to Colombia for a visit, and they said when I'm eighteen we might go as a family."

Now and then one of Josh's friends asks him questions about adoption. Usually he doesn't mind answering them, provided the children are truly interested. When the questions become too personal though, like, "How come your birth mother couldn't take care of you?" Josh gets uncomfortable. "That's the hardest question to answer. It's something I think about a lot. I've decided that either my parents had too little money to bring me up and felt adoption would give me a better life, or that maybe my mother had no husband. I know a kid whose father no longer lives with his family. That boy's mother is having a hard time raising him alone. If my birth mother had kept me, the same thing could have happened."

Despite his many questions about adoption, Josh says it isn't an everyday issue for him nor a subject he thinks about that much. "I know my mother and father love me. They say it a lot. Even if they didn't, I can tell from how they act." Josh is more preoccupied with his other interests, especially sports. "Mom and Dad say I'm a born athlete because I keep winning ribbons and trophies for swimming and baseball. They think it's because I have particularly strong arms. But truthfully I work hard at sports, and the awards make me feel proud," Josh explains.

Last year in school, Josh also earned the title of the class clown. He went as far as playing jokes on his teacher. Luckily his teacher had a sense of humor.

"I'm a lot calmer now than I was. But I still think it's important to have fun. I'd rather be more like myself— the kind of kid who makes people laugh—than a real studious workaholic. I'm the type of person I'd want most for a friend."

If wishes could come true, Josh says he would like to have lots of money when he's older and also be taller than he is. "I'm an okay size now, but I'd feel better being much bigger as an adult. If I could have been born from Mom and Dad I'd feel the best."

Still, for his own family, Josh plans to adopt as well as have biological children. "When I grow up, I want to have a few kids, and I'll do lots of activities with them. We'll play catch the way Dad plays with me, and we'll have chess games like Mom and I have. Definitely, I'm going to make a tree house with them. That's something I've always wanted to do with my dad. I think doing things together is most important for families. Also I hope my children like to joke and have fun. Then we'll really have a good time.

"In a way, adoption is the same as being birthed. There are different ways to build families. Giving birth is one way. Adoption is another."

"From the beginning, my parents made me feel adoption was something terrific"

CHRIS, age 36

"Although I don't remember my early childhood, I was born in France and lived in a foster home until I was two and a half," Chris says. While she was in foster care, Chris's adoptive parents were in France, too—her father was stationed there as an American military officer. "Mom and Dad couldn't have children and decided to adopt. Once they saw me, they fell in love with me immediately. As they made plans for my adoption, they were told about another child, a three-year-old boy who was also waiting for a family. After meeting him, they decided to adopt the two of us.

"My brother, Patrick, and I are not biologically related, but we resembled each other when we were young. People said we even looked like our adoptive parents. Although we could have kept our adoption a secret, we never did. Why would we?"

Soon after Chris and Patrick were adopted, the family got ready to sail to the United States. Before they left, French newspaper journalists and photographers came to interview them and take their pictures. "The French people treated us like celebrities. A few years ago, Mom gave me all the clippings from the papers and also my French birth certificate, which has my biological mother's signature on it. I've mounted everything in a special scrapbook that has memorabilia from my earliest days with my adoptive parents," Chris explains.

Chris's parents have told her that immediately after her adoption she called them Mommy and Daddy. Even today, being adopted gives her a good feeling. "It's something I've always been proud of, and I attribute that to my parents, who made me feel my adoption was terrific. Anytime the subject came up, they talked about it positively. Other people we knew made a fuss about it, too, and I enjoyed this extra attention.

"I liked being adopted because it made me stand out. While most kids don't want to be different—they want to wear the same clothes as their friends, eat the same food for lunch—I enjoyed being the unusual one. Even today adoption makes me feel unique in a positive way."

Chris has many fond memories of the things she and her family did together, particularly outdoors. "Mom was great in gardening, and I used to help her. Even today she and I plant together. The four of us were also animal people. Our family always had a cat or a dog about, in addition to sheep, chickens, and pheasants. After Dad retired from the army, he worked with the state police, but at heart he was a farmer.

"When I was about eight, Dad bought Patrick and me our own horse and built a large shed and a corral for it. He taught us how to feed and groom the horse, then he bought us a saddle and taught us how to ride. I really enjoyed that.

"On summer weekends Dad and I went fishing in a rowboat on a nearby lake. Usually we caught sunfish, which Dad showed me how to clean, and Mom cooked. More than the fishing, though, I enjoyed the quiet and calm of being on the water."

At the same time, Chris also pursued her own interests. "I was a tomboy as a kid—I played ball games against the school building and pitched marbles—but I also liked being by myself, doing things that made me feel peaceful—taking walks on a country road or writing poetry."

As young children, Patrick and Chris were staunch allies. Although they rarely confided in each other, they were protective of each other the way many brothers and sisters are. But as they got into the higher elementary grades, they started drifting apart. "From the very beginning I excelled in all subjects, but Patrick had difficulty with practically everything. He found ways to get out of doing his assignments, while I begged the teachers for extra homework. Since the two of us were nearly the same age, we were in classes together, which made it harder. Worse, Patrick knew how much Mom and Dad were pleased with my achievements and how they bragged about me to their friends."

To add to the friction, Patrick was uncooperative about household chores. "I can't say I liked them either. When it came to weeding the garden and taking care of the horse, I was willing to pitch in. But I despised having to be part of spring-cleaning and helping fix up the house on weekends. I wanted to be with my friends, going to the movies or just hanging out together.

"But my parents seemed to enjoy hard work. To them work was pleasure. Patrick, in particular, resented the household duties expected of us. But I did what I was told. More than anything, I tried to avoid getting into trouble. Like most kids, I hated having my parents upset with me. Of course that happened from time to time, but I found all kinds of ways to minimize it."

When Chris was thirteen, her father died. Soon after, her mother's sister came to live with the family. "Aunt Vivian was great. Of all my relatives I liked her best. Every summer, before she came to live with us, I visited her for a few weeks. Sometimes Patrick came along, too, but I liked it most when it was just Aunt Vivian and me.

"My aunt was the mail carrier for a rural town in New Hampshire, where she lived. I remember going with her in her jeep to make deliveries. She let me put the letters in the boxes. After work Aunt Vivian and I went to a nearby farm to buy milk which came in glass bottles that had a special part for cream at the top.

"In Aunt Vivian's house, the refrigerator was too old-fashioned to keep ice cream frozen. So every night we'd buy a small container of it, which we ate as we watched TV or played Parcheesi.

"Other than Aunt Vivian, none of my relatives spoiled me while I was growing up, and I really didn't feel close to most of them." Chris's parents were in their mid-forties when they adopted her. Both sets of grandparents were dead by the time she joined the family, and all her cousins were much older than she. "It didn't help that my family was scattered all over the country, which made it hard to visit one another."

After graduating from high school (she was class valedictorian), Chris went on to college and became a children's librarian. Now she is married and has two children, a boy and a girl.

"I'm happy with my job, especially since it allows me time to spend with my kids. I have a lot of fun with them. We play basketball together, and I constantly read to them. As an adult I see how much work there is to do around the house, but I make sure to enjoy my kids first," she explains.

Until she became a parent, Chris had no strong feelings about meeting her birth mother. But once she had children she started thinking about how hard it must be for a mother to give up her child.

"In my mind, it must be the most difficult thing in the world to do. At the time I was born, my birth parents were art students in college. When I was quite young, Mom told me that particularly back then, people in France who had children out of wedlock were strongly encouraged to place them for adoption. So even as a youngster I believed that my biological mother would have kept me if she could," Chris says. "That's why I've never felt unwanted, which has helped me along the way.

"Recently I've thought about searching, but it would be hard for both my birth mother and me. After all, we're just strangers. Still I'm curious to know what she did with her life. As a kid, I liked to paint. Although I never had formal lessons, I have some talent. Maybe I inherited that from my birth mother. I wonder what else I got from her.

"Besides my children, I have no one else related to me by blood although I'm close to a lot of people. For that reason alone, meeting my birth mother intrigues me. I've not discussed this with Mom, who lives with me now, so I have no idea how she'd feel about it. For the moment, I have no plans to pursue searching.

"From the beginning, my parents made me feel adoption was something terrific. And that's what I still believe. Although I have biological children, I'd like to adopt one day. My children know I'm adopted, and it particularly fascinates my six-year-old son."

Even as an adult, Chris feels adoption makes her a

more interesting person. "I love to tell people I was born in another country and about my parentage. When I think about my adoptive parents, I realize that if it weren't for them, I wouldn't be where I am today. I'm a decent human being, I've had a good education, and I have so many interests. I've done well being adopted."

"Why can't everyone just accept that we look different?"

SHAKINE, age 13

Shakine was almost four years old when he was adopted. Although he doesn't remember it, before his adoption Shakine lived in the medical facility of a foundling home in New York City. He was born with spina bifida, a disability which has made him paralyzed below the waist. To get around, Shakine has to use leg braces. Right now he's being fitted for new ones, so he's confined to a wheelchair. "I've been thinking about giving up braces completely. With my wheelchair, I can move faster, and I don't have to worry about being off balance," Shakine explains.

In Shakine's family there are seven children. "Three are biological and four are adopted. Alex, who's now fourteen, was adopted first. Then I came. Although my sister Tawanda and my brother David are older than us, they arrived later on.

"I don't remember when I was adopted. It's something I don't ask many questions about, nor do I spend much time thinking about it. On a scale of one to ten, with ten as highest, adoption's on my mind at around one or two. Whenever I want to know something about my adoption I ask Mom, and she gives me the answers."

Shakine's mother told him that in the foundling home he and Alex shared the same room and played together. "Somewhere in this house there's a photograph of the two of us when I was an infant and Alex was around two years old. Of all my brothers and sisters, I've known Alex the longest. We do the most things together now, although he can be a real pain," Shakine jokes.

Whenever he has to have surgery or even go to the doctor for a checkup, Shakine gets frightened. "Alex is the brother who cares most about me at those times. I can tell because he teases me less. He told Mom that when he gets older, he plans to have a good job, so that he can build a house for the two of us to live in together. Like my parents, he doesn't believe that I can take care of myself.

"If I don't want to go someplace with the rest of the family, Mom and Dad get nervous about leaving me alone. Mostly they're worried that I'll get hurt when I cook. Before they go out, I give them a pep talk that I'll be safe. Now that they see that I can make bacon and eggs without help, I think they're calming down."

Although Shakine doesn't remember who told him

he was adopted, he thinks it must have been his mother or possibly the child-care worker from the foundling home who visited him during the first three years he lived with his family. "Anyway, it seems like I've always known about it. Besides, being adopted is something you can't hide in this family," Shakine laughs.

Shakine is black and his parents are Caucasian. His sister Tawanda is black, too; David is Caucasian and black; and Alex is part Puerto Rican and part Greek. "Because our family has so many kinds of kids in it, people stare at us when we're together. Now I don't pay attention to it, but when I was younger it bothered me more. I didn't like people announcing our adoption in public and then having to hear them discuss it. Even today, I get annoyed when kids in school ask me questions after seeing me with my mom. Why can't everyone just accept that we look different? If they ask me why was I adopted I usually answer, 'Because I was,' and that's that. Adoption is my business. Besides, I hate explaining."

For the past few summers Shakine's family has vacationed in Maine, where they have a cabin. Recently, the family permanently moved to that state. Almost immediately, Shakine noticed a change for the better in his life. "Before we moved, I pretty much hung around the house after school unless my parents drove me to the 4H club or things like that. It was hard for me to get to places on my own. I never went to visit kids, and

I didn't invite them over, either. Other than playing ball with my brothers, I stayed mostly by myself," Shakine recalls.

Despite his handicap, Shakine has been able to excel in many athletic areas. "What bothers me most is that I can't walk or run around with the other kids. In my old school, while everybody played basketball, I went to a special room to lift weights. In some ways it was good for me. I got to improve my upper body and can now bench one hundred pounds. Still, I didn't like having to go off on my own and not be with the rest of the kids. Now I have this real young teacher who's big on having me take part in group sports. If we play volleyball, she makes sure I play, too. When it's my turn to serve, someone tips my chair back so I can aim the ball better to get it over the net."

During basketball games, Shakine's teacher appoints him the referee. He likes that position because he can zoom up and down the court. "I admit I run over some toes, but usually not that often. Also I cheat by calling my friends' balls in, when they're not."

Shakine's handicap continues to dominate his life and arouse his strongest feelings. He believes his birth parents didn't keep him because of his disability. Thinking about that makes him angry. "Maybe my birth parents were just teenagers and couldn't take care of a baby. Who knows? One day I want to meet them, although it worries me that if I do, I might yell, 'Why did you give me up?'

"I have a bad temper," Shakine admits, "but I'm working on controlling it. For a long time I wasn't fun to be with. In third grade I behaved so badly, I had to be sent to a school for problem kids. My mom says I'm generally a good kid, but during those years I 'erupted.' "

Even now, Shakine "loses his cool" when he's frustrated. "Alex has this rotten habit of bopping me on the head when he passes by. Because I'm in a wheelchair, he knows he can get away before I catch him. That makes me so furious."

Because some of the adopted children in Shakine's family have serious behavior problems, Shakine at times wishes he lived with other brothers and sisters. "For some reason, all my adopted brothers and sisters get into trouble too much. They take up a lot of my parents' time and make it difficult being in this house. Compared to some of them, I'm an angel. At least I don't go around hitting people or throwing things. If it could be more peaceful in my family, I'd be much happier," Shakine confides.

"Mostly I'm a good kid, and Mom says I'm a nice person. But I'm not the kind of person who gives in first. I won't behave a certain way just to be liked. But I'm not a troublemaker either. Well . . . only a little," Shakine smiles.

If something really upsets Shakine, he talks about it with his friends at school. "I don't have a best friend, at least not now. Last year I had to stay in the hospital for the whole summer and I made lots of friends there.

One girl in particular was very nice. She showed me how to stay out of trouble by helping me get to class on time."

More and more, Shakine has been confiding in his parents, too. For the past year or so, he's been telling them what's bothering him at school and what's worrying him at other times.

"I talk to Mom the most, but I like being with Dad the best. We don't have to do anything special. I just like being with him. Sometimes we go fishing together, but I don't even have to do that to have fun," Shakine says.

Because of his disability, Shakine's not exactly sure what he wants to do when he's grown up. "If I wasn't in a wheelchair, maybe I'd be a policeman. I love bossing people around. 'Move your car *now* or I'm giving you a ticket,' I'd say. More than anything, I want to drive a car. I'd love to get my license when I'm sixteen and get a nice red Porsche for my birthday," he teases.

At the moment, Shakine's more interested in what's going on in his life right now. He's working hard to get his grades up so he can spend more time at afterschool activities. "If my report card isn't that great, Mom and Dad don't make a big deal, but this new school is strict in that way. I really want to go to the afterschool basketball games and the dances, so I better improve my marks."

Lately Shakine's interested in improving his appearance, too. "My sister Maria, who's sixteen, has been giving me advice on how to look better. She tells me which of my clothes match and what outfits look best on me. Since coming to this new school, I'm more serious about my dress."

When Shakine is older he'd like to have two children, both boys. He says girls are too picky about everything. "I doubt if I'll adopt. In my family a lot of the adopted kids are hard. At least that's the way I see it.

"But me—I'm a winner. If I had kids, I wouldn't mind if they were like me—especially if they liked to fish and to joke," Shakine concludes.

"Underneath we know
we're all the same"

JAMIE, age 24

"In my family five children are adopted and two are biological, the oldest and the youngest. Mom is a diabetic and had trouble during pregnancy, so after my oldest sister was born, she and Dad decided to adopt. When I was four years old, Mom became pregnant with Robin, my youngest sister, and had to spend almost all nine months in bed. Robin's the one I'm closest to," Jamie says.

Jamie explains that each of the adopted children in her family was considered "hard-to-place" by the agencies. "All of us are part white and part something else: Chinese, Sicilian, Korean, and Mexican. I'm black and white. My adoptive parents are Caucasian."

Jamie's parents adopted her when she was five weeks old. As long as Jamie can remember, the family has treated adoption as an open subject. "Somebody was always asking where we children came from. As little kids *we'd* even get confused as to who was adopted and who wasn't. One of us with brown skin would ask our mother, 'Was it me who was adopted?' Or Robin would ask if it was she.

"In our home, being adopted never made much of a difference. If brothers and sisters yelled at each other, it had nothing to do with color or how you came into the family. Of course having so many brothers and sisters in a similar situation made it easier.

"Everyone in the house had to do chores, and the chores were unisex. Dad cooked and did the dishes and so did Mom. Both of them took the car to the shop to be fixed. We kids had our responsibilities, too, like washing the bathrooms or sweeping up. If one of us misbehaved, that person had an extra chore but never got a spanking," Jamie recalls.

Jamie's father, a minister, devoted his time to the church while her mother took care of the children. In later years, when her father became ill, her mother gave the sermons. "Mom and Dad brought us up to be compassionate people. I wouldn't dream of being anything but kind to others regardless of who they were or what type of problems they had.

"My parents have always accepted their children and loved them for who they are. Each of us kids was taught to get along with the others no matter what our skin looked like. Underneath we know we're all the same," Jamie explains.

Even so, as she was growing up, Jamie realized that sometimes she used her adoption as an excuse. "It seemed the easiest thing to put the blame on. I particularly recall one occasion when I resented doing chores my sister Robin was excused from because she had allergies. I yelled at my parents, 'You're making me do this because I'm adopted,' although I knew that wasn't the case. I understand now it's not unusual for adopted kids to use their birth circumstances as a tool, while biological ones might complain that they have it hardest at home for opposite reasons."

From the stories Jamie's parents tell her about her early childhood, she admits she wasn't that easy to raise. "Actually I was the terror of the family—into or under everything—the cabinets, the medicine box, the kitchen counters. As a little one, I'd walk out the front door all by myself and race down the street. It makes me laugh when I think about it.

"At around eight or nine years old, I remember I threatened to run away from home. Although I don't recall what made me angry, it must have been something serious. Anyway, when I told Mom I was leaving, she said, 'Make sure you take warm clothes.' Then she added, 'Who will feed Sasha (our dog), if you're not here?' Mom knew just how I would respond. And she realized I would never leave the family. Once I had calmed down, she comforted me. She always knew how to make me feel better.

"Even today, if I'm down I still turn to my parents.

They have a knack for soothing me. I think it's their optimistic outlook that cheers me up.

"Basically I'm a good person, and that's how I've always been. I try to please people by working hard to do things right. While I don't mind doing favors for others, I get real upset when they don't appreciate my efforts. I don't think this part of my personality has anything to do with being adopted. It's just who I am."

Until last year Jamie hadn't given too much thought to her biological parents. "From the time I was little Mom and Dad told me that my biological father was of royal Nigerian descent and that my mother was blond and blue-eyed. They had met in college but for some reason couldn't get married.

"Dad said that my birth father was the son of a tribal prince. He used to tease me by calling me 'Princess.' Since I liked the story, I've repeated it. But I don't know whether or not it's true."

A few years ago, Jamie wrote to the adoption agency that placed her, hoping they'd supply her with more information about her past. The little she got didn't help her much. "I feel like a cereal box with no ingredients. Even my furniture has a tag that says what it's made of. And written on the tag is, 'Do not remove.' I don't understand why adoptees can't know about their beginnings. I love my parents a lot. Asking questions about who I am won't take that love away," Jamie insists.

On her twenty-third birthday, Jamie suddenly wondered if her birth mother might be thinking about her.

"Possibly because I'm getting older and closer to having children, I realize how hard it must have been to give me up. I don't blame my birth parents for what they did. It must have been traumatic for them. If I could, I'd let them know I landed in a marvelous family," Jamie exclaims. "At this moment I don't find searching an attraction, and I don't know if I ever will. Mom and Dad are my parents. I love them. And I'm content with myself."

Because her parents feel secure themselves, Jamie says, her questions about adoption don't threaten them. "If I wanted to find my birth parents, that would be okay. My parents don't view searching as a kid's plan to run off with a new mom and dad," Jamie explains. "I'd like to have more information about my background. Do twins run in my family, for instance, or diseases like alcoholism? Not knowing the answers makes me feel deprived."

As an adult Jamie is more eager to tell people she's adopted than when she was a child. "I love to talk about my family. We're so neat. When I mention the adopted kids, I colorfully describe them, rattling off the different nationalities. When it comes to my parents and the two biological kids, I don't mention their background. I say, 'Oh, yeah, they're just plain,' " Jamie says, laughing.

Jamie has fond memories of being part of a large family. "I grew up in a fun environment. Even though we had little money, we did a lot together. And there was always someone to play with. It used to be a riot when Dad wanted one of us to do a favor and went through the whole list till he got to the right name.

"Today, two kids are teachers, and one brother's in the air force. Robin's now in college, majoring in international studies. It makes me proud to think that *my sister* is studying different cultures, just like our family. A few weeks ago, she came to visit me. When I introduced her to a fellow I know at work, he looked hard at her and said, 'Your sister?' I answered, 'Yes, my sister!' Robin and I laughed about it later. It's amazing how some people don't think about adoption."

Jamie feels that adoption has made her family even better. "To me adoption is an asset. In my family it didn't matter if my parents and I weren't of the same race. I never felt I had to explain my dad or mom to anyone. My parents took on more challenges than most people. They were a couple who created two babies and then also created by adopting."

"For me, the weirdest part of adoption is knowing that my birth parents might be alive"

AMY, age 12

"When I was six weeks old, my parents flew to Ecuador to get me. For half a year, Mom and Dad had written and talked on the telephone to a woman in Ecuador named Judy, who helped people adopt babies. One day Judy told them about me, and almost immediately, my parents were on the plane. They stayed in Ecuador for three weeks until the paperwork was finished and my adoption was made legal. Then my parents and I flew home together.

"I was a real cute baby with fat cheeks, dimples, and not that much hair. My eyes were as big and dark as they are now. I like to look at the pictures of me when I was little."

Today Amy has dark, shoulder-length brown hair. The bangs on her forehead curl up in humid weather. "Since my hair's dark and my skin's tannish brown, I look different from the rest of my family. Even though my brother, Jonathan, is adopted (he came when I was two), strangers usually think he's my parents' biological child because he's Caucasian like them. Actually, he only resembles Mom and Dad a little. Even so, Jonathan doesn't get the questions people ask me, like 'How come you don't look like your mom or dad?'

"In America I stand out, although not so much in school because many kids come from other countries— Korea, Argentina, Japan. But when I'm with my family, it's easy to tell I'm from somewhere else. Although I'm used to looking different, I don't always like it.

"I'm not saying I want to live in another town or with another family. I'm happy here with my friends and especially being in my house. And I like my family. When I get older, I hope I have a family as nice as mine."

When Amy was six years old, she and her brother were photographed for a book about adopted children. "Mom had told me about adoption before that," Amy recalls, "and I kept using the word, but I never thought much about it or for that matter where I came from.

"I can remember some kids in the playground telling me I looked like an Indian. I answered, 'I'm adopted,' but they didn't know what it meant. Since I was too young then to understand much about adoption myself, I couldn't explain it to them.

"But the day we went to have our picture taken, Mom discussed adoption with me again. This time I started thinking differently about it, especially when I saw the other kids who were also going to be photographed. I suddenly realized what adoption meant and that many kids besides Jonathan and I were adopted.

"For me, the weirdest part of adoption is knowing that my birth parents might be alive. Since Mom doesn't have any information about them, neither do I. Who knows why they gave me up? Ecuador's a poor country, so probably they had no money to raise me. Still, I wonder about my birth parents and sometimes thinking about them is scary. What if they want me back, like in the movie *Annie*? I spoke to Mom about this and she reminded me that she and Dad have signed papers that make me their child forever. Even so, now and then, when I'm not busy with other things, I think about what might happen to me. I rarely talk to anyone about these feelings, but they're inside me just the same."

Last year in school Amy wrote a report on Ecuador. Although she could have chosen any country in the world, Amy wanted to learn more about where she was born. "Mostly I wrote about Ecuador's geography, but just reading about the country and looking at pictures got me more interested in wanting to go there." And, she admits, she wants to see what the Ecuadorean people look like. "I wonder if a lot of them resemble me. Probably they do. Maybe I'd see my birth parents in a crowd." Recently Amy's parents told her that, in a year or two, the entire family will visit her native country.

This prospect reminds Amy of her feelings about a face-to-face meeting with her birth parents. "Although

I never want to get together with my birth parents," she says now, "I'm curious to know what they look like and whether they might be adopted, too. For some funny reason, I think they might be. Also I'd like to find out if I have any brothers and sisters. That would be neat."

Whether it's talking about her birth parents or troubles with her friends, Amy says that most often she confides in her mother. On a day-to-day basis, though, she gets along best with her father. "Dad and I play tennis together and he helps me with my schoolwork. Probably Mom understands me more than anyone else, but sometimes I think she can't see things from my point of view. That frustrates me. I hope one day when I have kids, I can imagine what's going on in their minds."

Amy admits that she gets frustrated easily, not only at home but in school, too. "Some days seem much harder than others. At times I have trouble falling asleep at night, worrying maybe because I couldn't do an assignment. Luckily my parents don't fuss if my grades aren't that good. And next year I'm going to a new school. Maybe things will go better there.

"I'm a really good athlete; sports are what I like most and what I do best. During the school year, I'm on the softball and soccer teams. In summer camp I play a lot of tennis and win trophies.

"My parents encourage me to stay involved with these activities since I am good at them and because sports are their main interest, too. Even my grandfather and my aunt are athletic. On February vacations, they come along with us when we go skiing."

Given the choice, Amy would rather spend her time with her family than with anyone else. "If my parents said we could do something special for the weekend, I'd give up my soccer or softball in a minute. I like it when the four of us go off together."

When there's no school, during Thanksgiving and Christmas holidays, Amy and her family travel to Chicago or California to visit their relatives. There she gets to see her cousins, whom she loves to be with. "Some of them, who are much older than my brother and me, really spoil us. It's too bad so many people in my family live far away—all over the country. It's hard if you want to have big gatherings, which I really like. At least I know that on April 29 everybody in my family will be together. That's my Bat Mitzvah date. I can't wait."

Since Amy enjoys being with people, she hopes her future job will be one where she can help others. "At times I'm sure I want to be a ski instructor or a tennis pro because I like the idea of teaching. Other times I think about being a therapist. Although now and then I'm quiet and shy, I'm a good listener. If I were a therapist, people would tell me their problems and then I could help them feel better," Amy explains. "It would be great if I could help people all over the world.

"My parents help me when I need them. I may not have come from Mom's and Dad's bodies, but they love me a lot. I always want to stay with them. They're my family."

"I wanted to see a face that resembled mine"

MARSHA, age 42

"Until I was seven years old, I was a happy-go-lucky child. I can tell from looking at our family movies. One of them shows me in preschool as queen of the May Day festival, wearing an elaborate costume. Seeing myself that way makes me laugh.

"Those were the times when I loved spending the weekend at my grandparents' house. Early in the morning I'd crawl into their bed and listen to Grandma tell me pretend stories about an ideal little boy and girl. Years later I told those same tales to my daughters.

"Life seemed so simple then. I'd go to school, then afterward Mom would take me shopping for a purse or a hat at my father's store, or we visited relatives who lived nearby. Later when Dad came home from work—he owned ladies' clothing stores—I'd climb onto his lap, and he'd read me the comics."

37

Marsha and her brother, Jeffrey, were particularly close then, too. "When we were younger, we mostly enjoyed imaginary games. One time our basement flooded, so Jeffrey and I got into a metal washtub and pretended we were at sea. During that period I remember spending hours drawing elaborate maps, which I explained to Jeffrey before we went on our make-believe trips. Even as we became older and grew more apart we still liked playing together, mostly building clubhouses on the back porch or in our basement. Half the time Mom couldn't find us."

Soon after Marsha entered second grade a classmate told her where babies grew in a mother's body. She immediately ran home from school to ask her mother if she came from her womb. "Mom said I didn't and went on to explain adoption to me. Nothing could have stunned me more. Up until then I had felt totally a part of my family and especially loved by my grandmother. Suddenly everything seemed different. Worse, I thought no one else in the world had begun life the way I did."

Years later, Marsha talked about that eye-opening day with her parents. "Mom remembered my screaming at her and Dad, 'You're not my real mother and father. I won't do anything you say.' Then I told my brother, who was three and a half at the time, that he was adopted, too, which he was."

Looking back, Marsha does not think her parents intentionally hid the truth from her. "More likely they were waiting for the right moment to bring the subject up, if there ever is a right moment. Too bad it had to happen the way it did. When adoption is an open topic, it's much easier to deal with.

"But at that time it was fashionable to keep it a secret. I think people felt uncomfortable saying they couldn't have biological children. My parents were even uneasy discussing my adoption with their best friends, who had been around when I came home from the hospital at two weeks old."

When Marsha heard about her adoption, other big changes were occurring in her life. "Besides finding out about my adoption, so much else happened to me that year. First we moved. Then I enrolled in a new school. It was difficult enough being the youngest child in my class, but I had to struggle to keep up with the other kids. Maybe I had a learning problem, too. Anyway, I started believing I was a beat behind everyone and soon pegged myself as stupid. While everybody worked in class, I doodled and daydreamed."

Marsha remembers thinking about adoption a lot at this time. But whenever she asked her parents and even her pediatrician specific questions about her beginnings, she sensed they were trying to avoid the subject. "Pretty soon I got the message that adoption was something very private. I wouldn't even discuss it with my brother.

"When I was nine, I overheard Jeffrey talking about

our adoption with a family friend. I quickly took him aside and reminded him not to share that information with anyone else. Until college, I kept that part of me a secret from all of my friends. Probably they never would have learned about it, except that one of my roommates was writing a term paper on the subject, and I spoke up."

Although Marsha felt close to her family during her growing up years—"It was obvious Mom and Dad loved me from the way they acted, and I loved them, too"—she began to believe her adoption must be affecting her parents' attitude toward her.

Looking around, she saw how frustrated they were when Jeffrey had problems in school. "My brother behaved badly and got poor grades. This caused many arguments with Mom and Dad." The only other adoptees she was aware of were her male cousins who, oddly, also had school or behavior problems. Marsha knew her aunts and uncles were discouraged over their children's troubles. Because she, too, did poorly in school—though her grades were her only downfall—Marsha became convinced that all adopted children couldn't measure up to their parents' expectations.

"I was pretty, talented in art, and popular with the kids. But I didn't believe in myself. Because of my poor grades, I felt my parents were disappointed in me. Of course I never told them this.

"Instead I became the good girl, hoping then my mother and father and everyone else would like me. I acted like an angel at home and in school, forever apologizing to people and saying, 'I'm sorry,' whether or not I was wrong. Nobody ever heard *me* lose my temper. I was the sweetest thing you ever met. People nicknamed me 'Marshmallow.'

"Today I realize that kids, biological or adopted, don't always have the same goals or interests as their mothers and fathers. I wish I had known that back then. Maybe I wouldn't have blamed all my shortcomings on my adoption. It became my main excuse when things went wrong."

The older she got, the more curious Marsha became about her birth parents. "My looks were different from Mom's and Dad's. They had dark eyes while I had large blue ones. And I was the only one in the family with red hair. I wanted to see a face that resembled mine. If I was in a crowd I stared at people, thinking one of them might be my mother. When I asked Mom and Dad for information about my biological parents, they said they knew as little as I and that the adoption records were not available to us. I accepted that for many years, but deep down I had many unanswered questions."

After graduating from college, marrying, and having two children, Marsha made up her mind to search for her birth mother. "Having my own kids made a big change in my life. I realized how much I loved them and how hard it must be to give up a child.

"My younger daughter resembled me and I wondered, did my birth mother and I look alike too? As soon as I told Mom and Dad my plans to find my birth mother, they said they would help me as much as they could. And they did."

Much to her surprise (and thanks to the special efforts of a worker in charge of the records), Marsha located her birth certificate and her birth name in a relatively short time. A few months later, with the help of a private detective, Marsha found out where her birth mother was living. "All the while, I wasn't exactly sure what I was looking for. Mostly I was curious to find out why she put me up for adoption.

"The night I called my birth mother, I mainly wanted to assure her I had turned out all right. There again, I was being the good girl.

"At first when I told her who I was, she denied being my parent and said, 'I can't help you.' " After Marsha's biological mother finally admitted the truth, she described the circumstances surrounding Marsha's birth.

"At the time I was conceived my birth mother was married to another man, who was in the army. To save her marriage, she placed me for adoption, but later got divorced anyway. She said I was her second child and that she had three more children after me. When I asked her who had red hair, she told me, my father. And she added that artistic talent ran in the family and wondered if I had it, too. I said I did. Besides that, we had little to say to each other. She didn't seem to want to talk much.

" 'Wait until your father hears about this!' she said,

before hanging up. 'He was the love of my life. We still keep in touch.' At least I felt comforted knowing she loved the man who fathered me. For so long, I had weird fantasies about my beginning."

All that following weekend, Marsha waited for her father's call. It never arrived. Nor did her birth mother ever try to contact her again. "During the year, I sent her a picture of my family, hoping she'd send back a photo of herself or at least write a letter. I wanted something from her that I could hold, if only a paper with her handwriting on it.

"A year later, I called again. Her voice had a cold tone. Now, in a way, I'm not anxious to meet her."

Although Marsha has spoken twice to her birth mother, she still has many unanswered questions. "For one thing, I know nothing about my medical background, but I'm not going to press my birth mother to give it to me. I've got to respect her privacy. Putting me up for adoption must have been hard for her in the first place, and now maybe she'd like to forget it ever happened.

"I know I ought to give up the search, but I'm not completely ready. I want to know some more about my siblings, and I'm curious about my heritage. All my birth mother shared about herself was that she's from the Midwest. I never even found out if we resemble each other."

For now, Marsha's keeping her birth mother's name and telephone number in her address book, and she's going no further than that. "The search hasn't worked for me. At this point I'm trying to move on."

Despite this setback, Marsha thinks she has gained from the experience. "It took me years to realize I'm made up of many parts. Adoption is only one ingredient. My personality has been shaped from living with my parents, from what I inherited, and some, just because I'm me."

Locating her birth mother has, if anything, improved Marsha's relationship with her parents. "I adore Mom and Dad, and nobody had better say a bad word about them. When I visit my parents, people tell me my father's face lights up the moment I enter the room. Before I leave, my parents ask when they're going to see me again. I know they love me."

Lately, Marsha has been concentrating on the good side of being adopted and even jokes about it. "One day when I was a teenager, I poured out my heartbreaking story to my grandmother. For a moment she looked at me, puzzled. 'I had forgotten you were adopted,' she finally said.

"It was so wonderful that she wasn't obsessed the way I was. She's that kind of person. We have a special love for each other."

Today Marsha thinks being adopted has helped her to become a stronger and more sensitive person. She has also noticed that people find it easy to confide in her. "Friends who've adopted children come to me when they have problems. They say they feel comfortable sharing their thoughts with me."

"For the past four years, I've been in therapy, working on getting out my anger and recognizing what talents I have to offer. I love my kids, and I have an adorable husband. From the way things are going, I can only guess they'll get better and better."

"I wish Mom was my biological mother"

MELISSA, age 11½

"Before I was adopted, I lived with my biological mother for six years. But when the courts found out that my stepfather and his son were abusing me and two of my three sisters they put us with foster families. In less than one year, I stayed in seven different homes," Melissa recounts.

Toward the end of that year, Melissa and her youngest sister, Joanna, were adopted by one family and their middle sister, Lara, by another. Misty, the eldest, who was already with their grandmother in Texas, continued to stay there. "Misty had lived with Grandma since she was an infant because our mother was unable to care for her," Melissa explains. "On and off, I got to see her, when she visited for the day or slept at the house. Although I was young then, I can remember giggling together with her at night."

The abuse of Melissa, Joanna, and Lara went on for several years before they were removed from their biological family. When Melissa was about two years old, her father died. He was Lara's dad, too. Soon their mother remarried, and a short time later Joanna was born. Then the abuse began. "My stepfather touched my sisters and me in places he shouldn't have. He hit us, too, and so did Mom. My stepfather was also an alcoholic.

"For some reason, which I don't understand, Mom brought me and not my sisters to a shelter where I'd be protected." Being alone in a strange place frightened Melissa, who's tried to forget about that particular experience. "Even when a neighbor was able to have Joanna and Lara sent to the shelter, too, I felt scared. I didn't know what was going to happen to us. In the shelter I became shy and refused to talk to anyone."

The girls were often separated when they were in foster care. "Lara and I stayed together a few times and Joanna and I, once or twice," Melissa recalls. "Some of the families I lived with were awful, but others were nice. A few even had pools so I got to go swimming a lot. One family tried to adopt the three of us, but they found it too difficult to manage us plus their own two children. Actually I'm glad *that* adoption didn't work out. I wasn't fond of the family."

Melissa's adoptive parents originally planned on adopting only one child—Melissa. When they heard there were two other sisters waiting for placement, they started to think differently. Because Joanna was only three years old, the adoption agency suggested to Melissa's future mom and dad that the young girl would probably be more comfortable staying with one of her sisters. So Melissa and Joanna were adopted together.

"I'm happy Joanna's in my family," Melissa says. "Now and then she gets me in trouble, but mostly I trust her. We came from the same mother, but we don't look that much alike. I have blue eyes and light blond hair. Joanna has brown eyes and dark blond hair. Actually Lara and I look more similar. In the end, it doesn't matter whether or not Joanna and I are biological sisters. It's more important that I can depend on her."

Just before the adoption, Melissa's social worker made a picture album filled with photos and stories about her life with her foster families. "When I was first adopted, I used to look at the pictures all the time, but I don't anymore. They remind me too much of how I felt back then—like a person who almost couldn't survive. Now I'm with a family that makes me feel safe and secure."

Because Melissa and Joanna somewhat resemble their adoptive parents, strangers don't usually ask questions. Yet when the girls first joined their new family, Melissa told everybody her background. "It was hard for me to keep things in," she explains. "When I met new kids I had nothing to say to them, so I told them about my life—not all the details, though.

"They'd reply, 'Oh, poor you.' Soon I started feeling sorry for myself. The more I talked about my problems, the worse I felt. It hurt thinking about how my biological mother didn't want her children and how she hit us a lot. I was even more confused because I was living with people who had wanted kids so much."

For a long time, even after her adoption, Melissa wished her biological mother had never remarried. That way, she thought, she and her sisters might have continued to live together with their mother in Texas. "We used to have fun there, swimming every day. Now that I've been with my adoptive parents for many years, I feel differently. Instead I wish Mom was my biological mother. It would be so much nicer."

Melissa also thinks about adoption much less than she used to. Although she hasn't forgotten about it, being adopted is something she's grown more accustomed to. "Most of the time I feel safe and secure here. That wasn't how it was before I arrived in this family. In the past I had bad dreams. Now I'm dreaming of happier things. What means most to me is having a family and lots of friends.

"Right now I don't have a best friend. The girl I liked most moved to South Carolina a year ago. I have other friends I hang out with, but they're not as much fun as Meredith was. Maybe that's why I miss my sister Misty so much. I'd like it if she were part of this family, too. When I was in foster homes, my three sisters and I would get together at the social worker's house for our birthdays. Misty was about eight then; now she's thirteen or fourteen."

Melissa imagines Misty as a teenager who would be going through the same things she's going through. She'd love to talk to her about social concerns, like boys. "It would be fun to have an older sister to confide in," Melissa says. "Mom doesn't understand every problem I have.

"For a while, I thought about writing to Misty or calling her on the telephone. But I realized that, if I did, my biological mother might find out where I lived. I don't want that to happen.

"Sometimes I bring up Misty in therapy. Every other Monday I meet with a group of adopted kids. We talk about what's on our minds. Since Lara lives nearby, she goes to the same group therapy sessions, and we get to see each other then.

"Joanna, Mom, and I also meet together with a therapist. Dad's at work at that time, so he can't attend. Usually I like the meetings with the kids better, but I go with Mom anyhow."

In school, Melissa is in the fifth grade, although she should be in sixth. Because she moved so often when she was in foster care, she needed an extra year to catch up. "At least I'm doing well, and my parents think so, too. I'm best in math, spelling, and reading. At home, I'm always in the middle of a book. And as soon as I come home from school, I do my homework."

When Melissa's much older, she plans to move to California and become an actress. This year she's trying out for a children's theater to see how well she does.

"One problem—I get shy in front of an audience. If I'm not an actress, I might become a beautician. I really like to style hair. Or maybe I'll become a lawyer and make lots of money.

"I'm smart and I'm proud of it. And I'm very thoughtful, too. I'm a good help around the house. Without being asked, I'll clean the rooms. I even help Joanna with her homework, even though I don't like doing it that much."

One day Melissa hopes to get married and have children. What concerns her is that, as a parent, she may act the same as her biological mother. "I don't think I'll lose control like my mother did, but . . . sometimes I lose my temper with Joanna. What if my kids upset me so much that, without thinking, I hit them hard? It worries me.

"Still, I want to have children when I'm older, maybe twins or triplets. Right now, though, what matters most to me is whether it's right for a girl my age to go on dates with boys. Mom says no. But kids in my class and I think differently."

Looking back over her life, Melissa says she has a pretty good one today. "Finally I'm in a real home. That's something I've dreamed about for a long time. If only my biggest dream comes true . . . to live happily ever after. Then I'll have everything I want most in the world."

"I liked my parents and wanted them to be my mom and dad from the start"

JOE, age 48

"Until I was forty-two years old, I refused to use the word 'adoption.' If it appeared in the morning crossword puzzle, I threw away the paper," Joe confides.

This anger began when Joe found out, at age four and a half, that he was adopted. Some children in the schoolyard told him. Probably they had overheard it from their parents. "That was not a good place to hear the news. I remember I ran home screaming, to ask my mom if it was true. She said yes. Then she explained that a few days after I was born, my birth parents were killed in an auto crash. A day or two later she and my dad heard about me. By the time I was one week old they had chosen me for their child. I was special, she said.

"Shortly after the revelation about my adoption, I had an eye operation, my paternal grandmother died, and then my mother gave birth to my brother. Two years later she had my sister. I thought these awful things happened to me because I was adopted. Why couldn't I have been born from my mother, too? I wondered. I liked my parents and wanted them to be my mom and dad from the start. More than anything, I did not want to be special. Being special singled me out."

Even within his family, Joe felt that he stood apart. His brother strongly resembled his father, and the whole family had black hair while Joe was blond. "Not realizing I was adopted, people would jokingly comment to my parents, 'Where'd he come from?' I wanted to hide."

For a while, Joe fantasized about living with other families. "In second or third grade, I imagined what it would be like having Sky King for my father. He was a radio character who was a rancher and piloted his own plane. I also thought about running away and starting a new life where no one would know my background."

When he was thirteen years old, Joe tried to keep his adoption secret from his brother and sister by burning the adoption books in the house. It didn't work. His sister found out anyway—from some children in the neighborhood—and his parents had already told his brother the truth a short time before. "It was bizarre that Mom and Dad didn't tell my sister anything until she confronted them with the facts. At least they told *her* all about my birth parents—that they were unmarried when they had me. I only heard about that six years ago. My sister was the source."

Immediately after Joe learned the complete story about his birth, he approached his mother and asked her why she had not told him the information as a child. "Mom replied, 'That's what we were told to say.' Then all my bad feelings about adoption made sense to me. No wonder for so long I buried the word 'adoption' under rocks with snakes and tarantulas. If adoption was something good, why would anyone, especially my parents, keep it a secret?"

Once Joe found out his parents were alive at the time of his adoption, "the biggest issue switched from being adopted to being given up. Every time I thought about it, I felt enormously angry."

Realizing that his birth mother might still be alive, Joe decided to search for her and joined a support group to help him in the process. Until then, Joe had never met or spoken to a birth mother. Suddenly he was sitting next to them at meetings listening to their stories. Soon he began to appreciate the difficulties they experienced, too.

"It's not easy being a birth mother and it's not easy being an adoptee," he says now. "Raising an adopted child can be a challenge for parents, too. Except for one other kid I knew, I grew up thinking I was the only adoptee in the world. Looking back, I realize I acted as if adoption was Mom and Dad's fault. Who else did I have to blame?

"For me the biggest fear as a child was that I'd be

abandoned again. Rather than admit this to anyone, I kept it to myself. Still, I had to make sure this would not happen, so I tried to be as obedient as I could. Actually I was too good. The only person I took my anger out on was my brother. When we were kids, my brother would move close to our mother and say, 'My mommy, not yours.' That hurt so much. Now I recognize that, at the time, he didn't even know I was adopted. My own insecurity provoked so many negative feelings."

With his sister, Joe acted differently. "I was eight years older than she and the firstborn, so she looked up to me. I liked being her big brother. When my sister was an infant, I remember how ecstatic I felt holding her, this gorgeous little baby with raven black hair.

"As she grew older, I enjoyed playing with her. In the summer when our family vacationed at the beach I showed her how to make sand castles. And when she got bigger, I let her use the control switch which made my electric trains stop and go."

Although Joe happily describes those times, he says he still felt on edge whenever the family went out together. "I kept thinking that a stranger might come over and ask, 'How come you don't look like anyone else?' That worried me along with being very small for my age."

After Joe told his parents that children teased him about his size, they took him to medical experts to see if anything was wrong. "The doctors said I was fine, but that didn't make me feel better. I still got teased. Instead of running around outside with other kids, I played alone with my dog or my chemistry set."

Luckily Joe's grandparents lived nearby, and the clothing store they owned was not far from his house. From first grade on, Joe went there straight from school. "I loved being with Grandma and Grandpa. Grandpa paid me ten cents an hour to do odd jobs, like picking up nails from the basement floor. Although I had a closer relationship with Grandma in later years, I favored Grandpa as a kid. He cooked the best chicken fricassee.

"That's not to say I didn't have good times with my parents, too. I'll never forget my seventh birthday, when Dad arranged for the two of us to fly over our house in a Piper Cub." And his parents were sensitive to Joe's fascination with anything mechanical. "As I was growing up my parents bought me electronic equipment and building sets, which I loved."

Even during these fun times, however, something seemed to dampen everything he did. If Joe and his father went fishing, he worried about killing the animals. When his grandfather took him to a chicken farm, Joe got frightened when the chicken nipped his finger. "I always had this feeling that things would go wrong for me." Joe realizes now that his main problem was a lack of self-confidence.

"Mom used to joke and call me 'Worrywart,' but she

didn't know how to make me feel better. Not until high school, when I got praised for doing phenomenally good class work, did I start developing a stronger self-image. About that time, too, I began a rapid growth spurt, which helped me think more positively about myself. At my father's suggestion, I then joined the wrestling team. That's when I started making friends," Joe recalls.

When it was time to go to college, Joe chose the one his father selected for him. "I wanted to please Dad, since I thought I was a disappointment to him because I was different from most kids I knew. He hoped I'd become a lawyer, though, like he was, but I said I wanted to be a nuclear physicist. In fact I became neither. While I was in college, my father died, and in the same year so did my aunt and uncle. Instead of finishing my schooling, I joined the army.

"A year ago, I finally got my college degree. Now I'm in graduate school and in two years I'll be a social worker. One day I hope to be a therapist and to open a clinic where I can help adoptive families work out their problems."

As for his own search, Joe is almost certain he's not going to find his birth mother. Now he spends little time on it. "It upsets me because I'd like to know where I came from. I'd also like to see if I have siblings.

"From way back, I've wished I had a blood relative, so I could look like someone else and also have roots. Like many adoptees, I feel as if I was never born—as if

I came from Mars. I'm curious, too, about little things, like what time I was born, and if I kicked inside my mother's tummy.

"As far as my birth father is concerned, I've not really thought about him. Maybe I'll meet him someday, but first I want to find my mother."

Sometimes Joe wonders what would happen if he did find his birth mother and she turned out to be very different from his fantasies of a wealthy, intelligent woman. Last summer, while he manned a booth about adoption, a bag lady sat down next to him and stared at him for hours. "All day long I thought, what would I do if she was my mother? I decided I'd take her to my home—with a clothespin on my nose. Then I'd put her in the shower. Afterward I'd give her a hug and see what happened next. What else could I do?"

With all that Joe has been through, he still feels very close to his adoptive family. "I'm the one who works hardest to keep us together. When my grandmother was dying, I flew to North Carolina to be with her. For me she was Grandma. She played an important role in my life."

Since Joe and his mother no longer have secrets between them, they've grown closer. "More and more I'm able to give my mother the affection I held back during all those years when I was angry. I was a difficult kid in all sorts of ways, but I've been making that up to her. Lately, our times together have gotten better and better."

And Joe and his brother are getting along well, too.
"Until two years ago, my brother and I were mortal
enemies. Recently we began having dinner together
every few weeks. Naturally we talk about our childhood.
I told my brother I was so jealous of him for being the
biological son. He replied that he was jealous of me
because I was the special, adopted child," Joe says,
laughing and shaking his head.

In other ways, too, family has become important to
Joe. Although he is divorced, he hopes to remarry one
day. "I definitely want to be a parent, and I don't have
to think twice about adopting a child.

"Six years ago, adoption wouldn't have even been a
consideration for me. But today I feel totally different
about the whole thing. I won't deny I want a biological
child, too, so I can have a blood-related connection. But
if that's not possible, I still want children," Joe says.

"For so long I fought being adopted, but now 99
percent of me accepts it. While in some respects, being
adopted feels different from being a biological child,
my adoptive parents are my family. I've never known
it any other way. If parents and children face the issues
of adoption it can work out."

"For a while I wanted my *real* mother and father"

MARK, age 10

"For the first four-and-a-half months of my life," Mark says, "I lived in an orphanage in Korea. Then my parents adopted me. Mom says that when I arrived, on September 19, my sister Katy's birthday and the day after my mother's birthday, I was like a present. Although I came sick and skinny, in a few months I had chubby cheeks and was real cute."

Besides Katy, there are two other biological girls in Mark's family. All are older than Mark. "I think Mom and Dad adopted me because they wanted a boy, and with adoption they could have a choice. That way Dad would have a son to play football with and take fishing. Now he has me and I'm happy to be of service to him," Mark says, chuckling.

"Of all my sisters, I spend the most time with Katy.

We're only two years apart, while Abby and Pam are fifteen and seventeen. But if any of my sisters hurt themselves, I'm there to give them a hand."

About two years ago, Mark says, he suddenly realized what being adopted meant. "It made me feel pretty queer—sort of weird inside. I started wondering if Mom and Dad were my real parents because they're not Korean. It made me angry when I realized they were not my birth parents, and for a while I wanted my *real* mother and father. Today I'm pretty happy with my family. But it's hard to be the only boy with three sisters," Mark says with a sigh.

"I don't exactly recall when my parents first told me I was adopted. I think I heard it when I was real young but didn't understand what they were saying. A few years ago they told me I was an American citizen, and I didn't know what that meant either."

Now Mark understands both concepts and he's happy about each of them. But at times he wonders what his life would have been like if he had stayed in Korea. Would he have felt more comfortable living with a Korean family?

"Luckily I have lots of friends, and many of them are also Asian. My friend Rui is Japanese, and I helped him learn English when he first came to this country. Now he invites me to his house and I like to eat there, especially when his mother makes Japanese pizza. It reminds me of the potato latkes we have on Hanukkah.

"Rui's mother teaches an enrichment course at school

that I take because I want to learn more about Asian cultures. She shows the kids how to do origami and make Japanese tops, and she teaches us how to speak and write in Japanese.

"Since Mommy has Korean friends I get to be with people from that country, too. On Passover, Mommy invited these friends and their children to our Seder so they could learn about our holiday."

Right now Mark's spending time with another boy who doesn't happen to be Asian. "Josh and I are both athletic and at recess we can always get into a soccer game. In school, when I have trouble with division, Josh comes over to my desk and helps me. Of all the kids in my class, Josh is the nicest. Everybody likes him—he's kind of a fad."

Mark thinks Josh probably knows that he's adopted, although the boys don't talk about it. "A few times in conversation with kids I've said, 'When I was adopted,' but I don't remember telling that to Josh. Since he's never been to my house and met my family, he may not even realize I'm adopted. I mostly talk about adoption with my family, either when we're all together at mealtime or when I'm alone with Mom and Dad."

One of the things Mark talks about is how it feels to be different. Because Mark is Korean and the rest of his family is Caucasian, he thinks he stands out in his family and elsewhere in the community. "Now and then kids at school insult me by calling me 'yellow.' I know people think Koreans are that color, but I consider my-self light brown or tannish," Mark explains. "Anyway, no one should name-call.

"Sometimes I hear bad remarks made about other nationalities, and I don't like that either. But when they're about *me*, I'm really bothered. For a while I thought that if I told kids I was Asian instead of Korean, their comments might stop. Instead they asked if I was Chinese or Japanese, making me have to explain fur-ther. If I had a choice, I would have been born Cau-casian like the rest of this family. Then it would be easier for me."

This year, Mark's mother became a foster parent to babies waiting to be adopted. By listening to the social worker's stories about each child, Mark has learned why some birth parents are unable to raise their children. "One mother and father were only fifteen years old—just teenagers," he recalls.

As for his own birth parents (about whom he and his parents know nothing), Mark has a few questions. "I'd like to find out how old they were when I was born and if they were hoping for a girl or a boy. Also I want to know the reason they put me up for adoption. Were they too young or too old? Were they too poor? I think they probably didn't have enough money to take care of me. If I met them—which I'm not sure I really want to—I wouldn't be angry with them. I have a family now and everything I need."

When the foster babies leave for their adoptive families, Mark says it doesn't bother him that much. "I pretty much like the babies Mom takes care of. When they're here, the whole family gets less attention, but it's not that bad. I don't mind doing things to make it easier. Sometimes I warm the bottle and then feed the baby or I'll hold the baby when Mom's busy. I wish we had a baby in this family to keep. Then I'd be the older brother instead of the youngest kid.

"Although I like the babies, when they go I'm not the one actually giving them up. My mother, though, gets so upset. She says she wishes she could keep them all.

"A little while ago, my great-grandfather, Pa, died. He used to come to our house for Passover every year. I liked *him* a lot. Seeing the babies leave isn't the saddest thing for me. What is, is knowing I won't see Pa again."

One of the reasons Mark enjoys the foster babies is that he likes helping people. He is especially eager to please his parents. "I try to behave well most of the time. That way everyone will be happy. If I help my parents I feel like I've done a good deed and have accomplished something. At times I give in the most in my family, but not always. My sisters act like princesses in this house, but I get my turn at being prince, too," Mark explains. "If I wasn't a good kid, I don't think Mom and Dad would let me have privileges like staying up late or doing something special with my friends. Anyway, when you act bad, your parents always get revenge."

Now and then, of course, Mark does misbehave. If his parents scold him, he sometimes wonders what it would be like to live with his birth parents. Or he thinks about changes he'd like to make in his adopted family. "First I'd want my parents to be less strict. In our house, no eating is allowed outside the kitchen. And Mom doesn't let me have TV games. Also I'd like not to have to do things just because my parents want me to—like homework. Ugh.

"In school I do well enough. Reading is my favorite subject. I loved *My Friend the Vampire* so much I read it eight times. Although my parents think I would do better in school if I worked harder, they were happy with my fourth-grade report card.

"When I grow up I want to be a lawyer, a doctor, or a scientist. But no matter what I am, I'll always find time to play tennis and take walks. Also, I plan to be as spunky as I am today, but I know I'll have to learn more self-discipline. If I'm a lawyer and I'm asked to play tennis while I'm in the middle of an important case, the game will have to wait."

Looking toward the future, Mark thinks he'll have children. He'd prefer two girls and two boys, biological and adopted. "If I adopted I'd ask for Korean children who have handicaps. Then I'd find them the best doctors and get them medicine so they'll be all better.

"One day, I really want a big family. It would be lots of fun except when I took them out for dinner. Unfortunately the bill might come to $140, and that might cost too much."

Mainly Mark wants his children to be happy with their family and get along well with their brothers and sisters. "Most of all I hope they'll like themselves and me, their father."

"Often as I grew up, I wondered, 'Do I belong here?' "

SAM, age 32

"Until I was six years old I lived in an orphanage in Korea," Sam explains. "As a young kid, I suffered from serious ear infections, which left me deaf in my left ear and hard-of-hearing in my right. In Korea, someone was always cleaning or examining my ears, which I hated 'cause it was painful. For some reason, the infections worsened. Finally the orphanage asked Welcome House, an adoption agency, to find a family who could get me the best medical care."

When the agency called Sam's future parents, they were not thinking about adopting. Besides having two high school-aged biological sons, they had just adopted an older girl who was part Korean and part Caucasian. "It didn't take long, though, for Mom and Dad to come to a decision. Mom said that once she saw my photograph her mind was made up."

Meanwhile the orphanage tried to prepare Sam for his life in America and taught him to write his name in English. "When it came time for me to leave Korea, I had no problem saying good-bye. Possibly because of my hearing loss, I had stayed by myself so much that I'd made no close friends or attachments," Sam confides.

Sam did not see pictures of his adoptive parents before he came to America. When his plane landed and a strange man appeared on board to pick him up, he wondered who it could be. "At first I was so frightened. Then I discovered the man was my dad."

Despite this rough beginning, it didn't take long for Sam to feel at home with his family. "Almost from the start, I considered Mom and Dad my real parents. This was easy since I hadn't known my birth parents at all. According to the records Mom and Dad received, I had been brought to City Hall—which in Korea is a safe place to leave children—right after I was born. Then I was taken to the orphanage. I'm not even sure if my Korean name, Si Won Lee, was given to me by my birth parents or someone at the orphanage."

Once Sam arrived in America, his parents immediately enrolled him in school, which he says helped him to adjust quickly to his new country. "I wanted to fit in, and being with American kids from the start forced me to do it. Since I couldn't speak English, I was placed in kindergarten instead of first grade. As soon as I caught on to the language, I stopped using Korean."

Because of his poor hearing, Sam had to have special

speech lessons throughout elementary school. These lessons particularly bothered him because, he thought, they further set him apart from the other children. From the moment of his arrival in this country, Sam knew he wanted to be an American. However, his obvious Korean heritage frequently made him confused about what place to call home. "When I was young, it was reverse discrimination. People went out of their way to be nice to me because I was different. In my family, I was the only full Korean, which made me proud. On the other hand, I always stood out. Often as I grew up I wondered, 'Do I belong here?'

"Since I adapted so quickly to this country and was readily accepted in my family, I thought I was so Americanized that no one would see me as any other nationality. That wasn't so, of course. Kids teased me anyhow.

"Sometimes I'd stare in the mirror and think I looked like my mother. I'm not exaggerating. I even developed her facial expressions. Then I'd go to school as the only Korean among four hundred kids and be singled out.

"During this difficult period, Mom helped me feel better about myself by creating a positive fantasy image of my background. In reality she knew nothing about my past. Mom said I must have come from royal and decent people who were leaders of an important village. She assumed that, she said, because I was a kind, caring person. Also Mom kept telling me I was beautiful. With her encouragement, I developed pride in myself, which helped me to handle the negative comments better."

By the third grade, Sam started catching up academ-
ically. Soon he moved to the highest track and stayed
at the top third of his class for the rest of his school
years. "There's a stereotype that Oriental children are
all bright. I was above average without studying, but my
main interest was sports—baseball, kickball, and
running.

"Although my father's a college professor and my
mother's a pianist, Mom and Dad never pressured me
to be a good student. They gave me opportunities to
learn, sent me to fine schools, and always had lots of
books available in the house. Yet, they accepted me for
who I was," Sam says admiringly.

Because of the great age difference between Sam and
his brothers and sister (the child closest in age to Sam
was ten years older), he didn't share many interests with
them as he grew up. Still, he felt he was a part of a
family unit. He liked that everyone usually ate dinner
together and went to bed at the same time. "But each
of us pursued our own interests, by choice. Still there's
no doubt in my mind that my heart's always been with
my family. In no way would I want anyone else's mom
and dad."

As a teenager, Sam had to grapple with his cultural
identity once more. "When I was younger, I didn't see
many other Koreans. In fact, I was the only one in my
town. The year after I arrived in America, my parents
took me to the Welcome House picnic for adoptees and
their families. I distinctly remember that day because

they served genoa salami, which reminded me of the spicy Korean food I had eaten in the orphanage. Other than that event, I can't recall having contact with Koreans or learning much about the country until college. As a kid I had totally identified with being an American.

"At age sixteen, though, I discovered that others didn't necessarily see me the way I viewed myself. When I asked blond, blue-eyed girls for dates, they turned me down. Here I considered myself as American-looking as anybody else, yet the girls I had always gotten along with rejected me. While all my friends were bragging about their dates, I couldn't say, 'Hey guys, look who I'm with.' My first reaction was to hate being Korean." It took Sam a long time to appreciate his Korean background. Only in the past few years has he felt proud of his dual heritage. "Finally, now, I recognize that the American and Korean parts of me overlap. For so many years I couldn't admit to that."

Seven years ago, Sam opened his own karate school, where he teaches adults and children the Korean form of the martial arts. After not speaking the language since he arrived in America, he now uses Korean words to give certain commands.

During the summer Sam also teaches karate at a camp for deaf children. "For three years after college I was a special-education teacher. Since the first part of learning karate is watching, children with hearing problems do especially well," Sam explains.

Although Sam feels he's accomplished a lot in life

through his own merits, he admits that his parents helped him in many ways. "From day one they accepted me and treated me like the other kids in the family. For that alone, I'm thankful. I've tried to be a good son to them, but like all kids, I had to grow up and develop on my own, too.

"I know my parents love me and are proud of who I am. My mother keeps saying I'm a good person. Still there's a part of me—maybe 1 percent—that thinks my parents will favor their biological children more in life. I don't know why I think that way. Perhaps all adoptees do.

"Recently I asked my parents to lend me some money for my business. When they refused, I admit that I blamed it on my being adopted. Later when I told my brother, my parents' biological son, about the incident, I discovered that he, too, had been turned down for the same request.

"When I'm feeling good about myself adoption is my friend. It makes me a more interesting person. But adoption can be my bitterest enemy, too, if I use it as an excuse for what I can't have."

Two years ago, Sam attended a Welcome House re-union, which was held for adoptees who were sixteen years old and up. It was the first time since that picnic many, many years before that Sam met adopted Koreans in a group. "By then I felt secure about myself and my business life, too. I also had positive feelings about being adopted. Out of curiosity I wanted to see how other adoptees turned out and whether they felt the way I did."

Like Sam, most of the people he met were happy with their lives and were eager to share their feelings and experiences. "It took me a whole year to absorb what I heard at that reunion. For a long time I hadn't discussed the subject of adoption with others. But today, if someone gets me on the topic, I can go on talking about it late into the night."

Another reason Sam found the reunion a success is that he met his future wife there. A year later the two were married. "Paige was adopted when she was eight. She has a photo of herself with her biological brother and sister taken before she left Korea. For me the hardest part of being adopted is that I don't know anyone I'm connected to by birth. When it comes to my looks, I have no one to compare myself to. One day, though, I'll have kids, and then I'll see some of me in them. Just thinking about it gives me goose bumps."

"When I grow up I'd like my family to be exactly like the one I have now"

DYLAN, age 9½

"I was two months old when I was adopted. My adoptive parents had wanted a baby for so long but couldn't have one of their own. Just as they were about to leave for a vacation, the agency called and asked if they wanted a child. Of course, my parents said yes immediately. Mom says they were very excited when I came home. From the pictures taken at that time, I can tell I was sort of cute," Dylan says proudly.

Right before Dylan's second birthday, his parents adopted his biological sister, Stacey. "I get a good feeling when I think about being related to Stacey. I like that she and I have the same color eyes and hair. Although her hair is real curly and mine is straight, when I was younger I had curls, too. Probably our birth mother also has curly hair."

Dylan doesn't remember exactly when or where he first heard about adoption. He guesses his mother must have explained it to him when he was very young, because in nursery school, he and his friend Katy liked to pretend they were parents of adopted children. At the age of four, Dylan thought adoption was the only way to have babies.

"Then when I was in kindergarten I finally understood what adoption really meant and that I was adopted. What a surprise! Before then I hadn't realized that adoption had anything to do with me. Maybe I didn't take adoption seriously when my parents first told me about it, or maybe I didn't listen very carefully," Dylan confesses.

Today Dylan does not dwell on the fact that he is adopted. He's more concerned about performing on stage in school or playing baseball. "One day I hope to make the Little League majors. Then when I'm older, I want to be a professional player and break Babe Ruth's and Ty Cobb's records. I'd love to be in the Baseball Hall of Fame. That would be great."

Given Dylan's attitude, most of his friends have found out about his adoption from others, not from him. "Some kids don't believe it because I sort of look like my family. When they ask me questions, I answer truthfully. I don't mind talking about the subject.

"Although I don't spend much time thinking about being adopted, I still wish I had been born from Mom.

Somehow I feel it would have been easier for all of us if my parents had me from the beginning. I can't exactly explain why. It's just something I believe.

"Awhile ago a girl named Mary stayed with us for a month until her baby was born. Mary was eighteen years old and not married. She had already decided to give up her baby for adoption."

When Mary went to the hospital, Dylan was in school. But days before the baby's birth he noticed that Mary was sad. "I didn't ask her why she acted that way, but I guessed it was because she wasn't keeping her child. That must have been a hard decision to make.

"About six months after the baby was born, our family went to visit the people who adopted him. By now Mary had moved far away. But I think she would have been glad to see that her child had a good mother and father to take care of him and that he and his adoptive sister looked so happy," Dylan says.

Since the family's experience with Mary, the subject of birth mothers comes up much more often in Dylan's house. Usually Stacey starts the conversation. "My sister's the one who has the most questions about adoption. Mom tries to give her as much information as she can but she doesn't know that much about our past. Mom told us our birth mother was fifteen or sixteen when I was born, so probably she was too young to raise us. Even when Stacey came, she was still a teenager.

"A few weeks ago, Stacey said she wanted to find our birth mother. Mom told her that when she's older, she'll help her get in touch with an agent who has the files. If Stacey meets our birth mother, maybe I'll go with her. Then I can ask exactly how old she was at my birth. It's something I've been curious about for a long time. Also I'd like to know what she looks like. I try imagining her face, but I can't figure it out. Probably she has blue eyes and brown hair like me.

"Mostly, I want to make sure my birth mother has a good job with enough money to take care of herself. I don't worry about it that much, but I think about it now and then," Dylan confides.

Someday Dylan hopes to have children. "I'd adopt and also have biological kids. First I want a boy who would be tall, then I'd like a little girl. She'd be the youngest, the way it is in my family. I'd act pretty much the same with my kids as Mom and Dad act with me. I'd read to them and play ball with them and take them to jazz concerts.

"When I grow up I'd like my family to be exactly like the one I have now. I hope I have good kids, too, who do their homework, practice their instruments, and keep their rooms sort of neat."

"Even though I've never met my birth parents, I still miss them"

STACEY, age 8

"I'm happy to be alive today. That's the most important thing. Mommy and Daddy tried to have babies but the babies couldn't live in Mommy's womb. So they adopted Dylan and me.

"Dylan came first. About a year and a half after that I was born. One day the social worker called my parents and asked, 'Do you want another baby?' They said, 'Of course,' so then my parents adopted me. I was seven months old when I came to live with them. Before that I had been with a foster family. Now my adoption is final because my parents went to court and signed the papers," Stacey explains.

"It feels weird when I think about Dylan and me having the same birth mother, but I'm not sure why. Mommy told me that in the olden days they didn't put brothers and sisters together. It's funny how my parents got to adopt the two of us. Anyhow, I'm glad Dylan's in the family. That way I'm not the only adopted child. Besides, I like having him for a brother . . . at least some of the time."

Most people who don't know Stacey's family can't tell that the children are adopted. "We almost look like our parents," Stacey suggests. "Mommy and I even have the same curly hair. Funny, that's the one part of me I'd like to change. I want waves that don't knot up and look messy when I brush them."

Once in a while when Stacey's parents tell their adult friends that their son and daughter are adopted, those parents tell their children. "Kids don't always believe what they've heard and ask me, 'Are you *really* adopted?' I just say yes, and that's that. It doesn't make me feel bad or anything.

"My best friend, Lisa, knows I'm adopted, but we don't talk about it much. We'd rather play rummy or jump rope together.

"Mommy told me that long ago parents kept adoption a secret from their children. That surprised me. I don't remember exactly when I was told I was adopted—I might have been a baby. Anyhow I've known about it since I was very young."

Stacey recalls the good times she had with Mary two years ago while Mary waited for her baby to be born. "We used to fix each other's hair, and Mary polished my nails. I liked having her here because she played with me. The day her baby came, Mommy and I took her to the hospital. Mary kept crying because she didn't want to give her baby away for adoption. When I saw how she felt, I was kind of sad for my birth parents, too. It must have been hard for them to give up their baby.

"A few times I've asked Mommy if she ever saw my birth mother, and she said no. It's funny, but even though I've never met my birth parents, I still miss them.

"I'm really curious about my birth mother. I wonder if she has the same coloring as Dylan and me. I can't imagine what she looks like. When I get older, I want Mommy to help me search for her. Maybe Dylan and I could go meet her together, but Mommy would have to come along, too. I know my birth mother lives in New York City, but I don't know her name. I'll probably find out when I'm eighteen."

If, in fact, one day Stacey does meet her biological mother, she's worried she might be embarrassed. "What if my birth mother doesn't recognize me? I look so different from when I was born. I'm also not sure if she'll like all the questions I have to ask. Mainly I want to know why she couldn't take care of me. Probably she'll tell me she was very young when I was born—still in high school. And she'll say she loved me and really wished she didn't have to give me away."

Today Stacey takes special pleasure in being with her family. "Last night a big tree fell on our road, knocking out all the electricity. To have some light, Daddy lit a kerosene lamp and put candles around the house. I loved it because it reminded me of the olden days.

"I also like when we go on day trips together. A few weeks ago the four of us went to Mystic Seaport in Connecticut with other families who have adopted children, too. The trip was arranged by the adoption organization Mommy used to be the head of. Now she's not so active, but she still attends meetings."

Although Stacey feels closest to her mother, she gets along well with her father, too. And she's also glad Dylan's her brother. "We may fight over who gets to use the computer first, but that's not a big deal. I'm happy he lives in this house. If Mommy and Daddy go out at night and don't get a baby-sitter, I feel safer if Dylan's there with me."

Even though Stacey says she doesn't dwell much on the subject of her adoption, she's still sensitive about it. This is especially true when she visits the school where her mother teaches. "When Mommy's students see Dylan and me they ask her, 'Are those your children?' They may be curious because they're not used to seeing us with her. But sometimes I really think they're wondering if we're adopted. That makes me feel funny—like people can tell things about us from just looking at our faces. At least I have parents and I'm not in an orphanage like Annie.

"I tell Mommy about my happy and sad feelings, and she's glad I don't keep these thoughts inside me. Mommy's the person I talk to the most. This year my friend Rachel died, and I was very upset. It frightens me that something might happen to me or my parents, too. I was in a car accident once but luckily I was okay. Then I fell off a ladder at school and broke the humerus bone in my upper arm. When kids laughed at me, I said, 'Well, it's not that humorous!' " Stacey giggles.

When Stacey grows up she wants to have $11 million so she can take her family to Disney World. She says she'll probably earn the money as a dancer on Broadway. "I don't take lessons yet, but at home, I create my own movements, and I'm good. That makes me happy, but not as happy as I feel being adopted and having my mom and dad. I'm most happy for that!"

"I had to make sure I was searching for the right reasons"

JIM, age 37

"I discovered I was adopted when I was thirty-three years old. By some strange coincidence, I met a man in a café who had been my neighbor when I was a kid living in Florida. When I asked him if he remembered me, he said, 'Of course I do. I drove you home from the adoption agency when you were just one year old.' At that moment I felt myself shaking inside. I couldn't believe what I heard, yet I knew it must be the truth," Jim recalls.

Until then Jim had no idea he was adopted. As a child, however, he felt as though he didn't really fit into his family. Although his looks weren't that different from his parents' (he had no brothers or sisters), that wasn't the problem. "Mainly I wondered why none of my relatives shared my interests. I couldn't find one subject in common with any of my thirty cousins. While I liked to do science and electronic projects, for example, they preferred building models from kits. We just didn't think alike. After a time, I avoided family get-togethers. You could say I was a loner. I felt more comfortable moving cows and riding horses on the New Jersey farm where I spent my summers than being with my family."

Today Jim thinks that this discomfort had to do with his being adopted, although many adoptees would point out that biological children can feel isolated from their family, too.

"Looking back, I realize that another strange thing signaled my adoption. When I was fourteen, Mom wouldn't let me visit my paternal grandma who was in a nearby nursing home. As a kid, I spent a lot of time with Grandma. Our houses were close to each other's and I'd run over to be with her all the time. Suddenly I was forbidden to see her. The more I pressured Mom to let me go, the more anxious my mother became. Finally she said Grandma was in bad shape and couldn't have company.

"Only now is it clear that Mom was afraid Grandma might tell me about my adoption."

Three years before this Jim's father died. When Jim was thirteen, his mother married a man who had been a friend of the family. "I got along better with my stepfather than I did with my father. My father had a hot temper, which he often directed at me. While Mom heard and saw what went on, she couldn't do much to control his behavior. For my own safety, I stayed out of his way as much as possible. With my stepfather, I felt totally relaxed. We did so much together. He took me on a trip to Italy and taught me about the history of the country. And at Christmas he helped me make toys. Before he married Mom, he asked my permission, which was neat. From the moment he came into the family, I called him Dad.

"Dad was with Mom when I confronted her about my adoption four years ago. At first she denied everything. 'No, it's not true,' she insisted. When I pressed her, she finally admitted it. 'Now that you know, does it make any difference how you feel about me?' she said. 'No, I still love you. You're my mother,' I replied. 'But why did you keep such a secret?' Mom had no answer. I don't think she knew the reason herself.

"Anyway I was very angry and confused. Suddenly I didn't know who I was."

Jim's mother tried to comfort him by showing Jim the court decree that said he was legally adopted. Also she told him what she knew about his birth and infancy: that he was born in Florida, had been in an orphanage, and at four or five months old was hospitalized with pneumonia. "As far back as I can remember I've always loved flying and eventually made it my profession. Yet I've never been able to trace the source of this fascination. Hearing I was in a hospital and an orphanage, I've guessed my crib was placed near a window where I could look up at the sky and watch the floating clouds. Anyway, it's a nice thought," Jim says, laughing.

With only that little bit of information about his life, Jim still felt lost. "I didn't know to whom I could turn, so I called a girl I had dated in high school who was also adopted. She was now married and had kids, but we still kept up with each other. As I drove to her house I thought, what if she's my sister? She wasn't, of course, but for the moment, the idea scared me."

Jim's former girlfriend couldn't advise him. "When I described how I felt being kept in the dark about my birth, she said, 'It doesn't matter where you came from. Be thankful for what you have.' That's not what I wanted to hear! I had hoped she'd sympathize with my wanting to know more about my background. But since she had no interest in discovering her own, she couldn't appreciate my feelings."

Jim's nonadopted friends didn't understand how he felt either. "They said, 'It's for your own good that your mother kept the truth from you. So you're adopted! What's the big deal?' Instead of supporting me, they sided with Mom."

Jim found he couldn't ignore his adoption. There were, he thought, special issues he had to deal with. "I had no family tree. Most people don't realize how much this comes up in daily life. Even though I considered my adoptive parents my mother and father, I still wanted to find out more about myself. Was I Irish, Jewish, or Italian, for example? What was my medical history? When my adoptive father had died of a heart attack at a young age, it worried me. Now, that wasn't part of my medical history, but what was?"

Jim wasn't looking for a replacement family—a new mom or dad. "I had good memories of my childhood. I can still taste the batter Mom let me lick from the bowl each time she made a chocolate cake. And I'll never forget the time Dad and I made a kite together and flew it over an enormous field near our house. That was a lot of fun. But I needed to pinpoint my beginnings.

"Then I found out about a support group of adoptees. At last, when I shared my experiences with them, I realized I wasn't alone. There were others in the group who had also discovered they were adopted at a late age, and they, too, had reacted as I did.

"The longer I attended group meetings, the more convinced I became that my feelings about search were natural. It gave me confidence to explain my attitude to my nonadopted friends who were urging me to give up the idea."

Jim was mainly interested in finding his birth mother. "My mother carried me around for nine months so she was the one I thought about more than my father. I wondered, was she a woman from a wealthy family who didn't want to embarrass anyone when she became pregnant, or was she some addict who could make my life miserable? Fantasies like these kept entering my mind."

Jim's mom was uncomfortable when he first told her he was searching for his birth parent. "Mom was scared

I'd stop loving her. I think at first she felt threatened. Probably that's the reason she didn't tell me about being adopted right from the start. It took me some time to convince her that looking for my birth mother had nothing to do with my feelings toward her. For a while, I felt guilty about hurting her, but then I realized this was something I had to do, and there was no stopping me. Eventually Mom became more supportive and told me, 'I guess you've got a right to know certain things.' "

Searching for his birth parent meant being persistent. Jim sometimes felt like Sherlock Holmes. "Every clue must be checked out. With effort and patience, pieces start fitting together like a puzzle."

In time Jim finally located his birth mother, and eventually they had a reunion in Maine, where she lived. "Although as a pilot I am accustomed to being prepared for lots of emergency situations, there was no way I could prepare for meeting my mother. No book had been written to tell me what to say or do. I had to play it by ear. My birth mother was as nervous as I. Her lip was quivering when she saw me.

"We hugged and nearly cried, and then we talked. She told me her life hadn't been easy. And she tried to reassure me that I wasn't rejected as a baby. When I was born, she was only seventeen. Instead of telling her mother she was pregnant, she went to Florida, got a job, and waited for my birth. Even her sister didn't know what was going on. 'I barely had an education or money to support you. I did what my head told me to do, but not my heart,' she said. Now my birth mother's married, has three daughters, and a nice job. She's good-looking and quite intelligent. More important, she's understanding and sympathetic."

Sometime later, Jim visited her again, this time for a weekend. "I met one of my half sisters and my eighty-five-year-old biological grandmother. My birth grandmother is the kind everyone would love to have—twinkling eyes, sharp, healthy. And I like my half sister too. Here I was an only child. Now I have three siblings."

Jim is satisfied with what he found. "Luckily things turned out pleasant for me. It doesn't always happen that way. In my case I didn't come from very bad folks or from royalty, just ordinary, decent people. I'm relieved to have ended my fantasies and I'm ready to get on with my life. Even Mom is comfortable with my new situation.

"Searching isn't for every adoptee. I don't recommend that people just go out and do it. You have to search with your eyes wide open. Possibly things may not work out well, and you must be prepared for this. I found it was important to talk to people—to get counseling—before I actually searched and while I was in the middle of it. I had to make sure I was searching for the right reasons. Some people go out and search because they're angry at their adoptive parents or for being adopted. If they find their birth parents and they're not happy with them, they may have bigger problems to deal with afterward."

However, Jim feels that even a bad reunion can turn into a positive experience. Children who are disappointed with their birth parent or parents may, he believes, become more appreciative of their adoptive mother and father. "If my birth mother wasn't all that great, I still would have come out ahead. I would have realized even more that being adopted gave me a better life than if I had stayed with my biological parents."

And searching has given Jim a personal history he felt was missing from his life. "It's important to have roots," he says. "I'm working to help change our country's laws so other adoptees can have access to their heritage, too."

Today Jim says he feels being adopted has been a plus for him. "I've had to deal with a lot of challenges in my life. As a kid, I didn't do well in school, my father died early, and then at a late age, I discovered I was adopted. For some these may be obstacles but they helped me mature. Talking to other adoptees and to birth parents and adoptive parents has put me more at ease. Now I trust people more and allow myself to get close to them.

"Since I've overcome a lot of my insecurities, I feel that I'm a better person. And I'm finally growing up. It's about time," he says, grinning.

"I'm finally home"

RENEE, age 8½

"In my family, there's me and Mommy. We play Barbie dolls together and like the same TV programs. When we go out shopping, people who meet us can't tell I'm adopted. We don't look that different even though Mommy has hazel eyes and I have brown," Renee explains.

"Although I've been living with Mommy for only eighteen months, it feels like we've been a family since I was a baby. When I first came to Mommy's house, I felt sure she would also give me up like the other families I had stayed with. When I told her this, she said to me, 'This family is it!' Deep down I'm starting to believe her."

When Renee was three-and-a-half years old, she and her older brother and sister were removed from their biological parents' home because their father had abused the children. For another three-and-a-half years, Renee lived with eight different foster families. "Sometimes I was separated from my brother and sister. Then other times we'd be back together again. Finally I was placed in the home I'm in now. My sister and brother are with different families.

"Still, we talk on the telephone and see each other a few times during the year. This summer we're going on a camping trip together. The adoption agency that placed us made all the plans for it."

After Renee was removed from her biological family, she lived with some families she liked a lot and others that were unpleasant. "One family worked in a graveyard, which frightened me. Another, which was nice, tried to adopt all three of us. My brother, sister, and I stayed with them for eleven months, but it didn't work out. Leaving that home scared me, because I wanted to be with that family so much. If I don't stay with Mommy, I won't forgive myself."

Renee also remembers the foster parents who abused her, just as her own father hurt her and touched her in private places. Because of these experiences it takes Renee awhile to trust adults. "Sometimes when Grandpa plays with me I get afraid. He'll say something which reminds me of my first dad and mom. I'm trying hard to get them off my mind, but it doesn't always work. When I get really upset and start crying, Mommy holds me tightly."

Renee says her mother adopted her because she always wanted a child. "Mommy says it didn't matter if it was a boy or a girl, as long as she had someone to love. Now she has *me*. And I have a nice mother, too.

"Mommy says she'll never give me up, not even if I drive her crazy. Once we sign the adoption papers, I'll feel better. The lawyer's been working on them for so long, and I'm getting impatient. I keep singing this song I made up, 'Take a short time. Don't make me wait. . . . ' "

Before coming to live with her mother, Renee had never attended school. At seven years old, she couldn't read or write her name. Now she's in a special program for bright children. "I do well in class, not great," Renee says. "Mommy says I could do better in behavior and on tests, especially math. Evey night she quizzes me on my numbers. I finally learned the times table, but I hated having to do all the work."

Mostly Renee wears a big smile and giggles a lot. She admits, though, her smile sometimes hides sad feelings. "I try to smile because it makes me feel good," she explains, "but it doesn't always work. I can draw a beautiful picture of myself getting ready to take a swim in the ocean. Without realizing it I've made dark clouds and raindrops above me. The raindrops look like tears falling down my face. I know it means I'm crying inside, and the sky is crying, too, because it doesn't like to see me sad.

"When I show these pictures to Mommy, she encourages me to get out my feelings. But I worry that if she sees me sad, she might feel unhappy, too. I don't like making people unhappy. And I don't want to do anything that might make Mommy want to give me up."

To help sort out her feelings, Renee talks to a therapist. Now she's beginning to like more things about herself. "I'm smart—I can even read well, and I have a pretty face. I'm definitely a nice person, too."

Being with all the people in her new family also makes Renee happy. "At first I felt strange. Meeting so many aunts, cousins, and grandparents for the first time was hard. It took awhile for me to get used to them, but now I like when we visit with each other. I've gone to Florida to stay with my grandparents, and I go to my cousins' houses, too. One of them lifts weights and carries me around like I'm nothing. Finally I feel I'm really part of a family.

"Still, I love my brother and sister and at times I miss them. It gets a little lonesome being an only child. Then I think back to the times my brother and sister hurt me badly, and I realize I'm better off being just with Mommy. Anyway, Mommy said she might adopt another child next year—a boy. That might be nice.

"When I told my best friend, Leslie, I was adopted, she said she wished she was, too. She thought it was kind of neat. But I said, 'No way is it fun to be adopted if you have to move from one home after another to get there. That becomes confusing, 'cause you don't know when it will stop.'

"Now at last I think I've come to the end of going from family to family. Everybody regards me as Mommy's daughter. That's a special feeling. It's like I'm finally home.

"When I get older, I'm going to have a good job. Maybe I'll be a teacher like Mommy or a vet. Probably I'd have to learn lots of skills, but if I really wanted to I could. When I make up my mind to do something, I can do it real well."

Like her mother, Renee doesn't think she'll ever get married. "It's easier that way," she explains. "But I'm planning to adopt kids. That I'm sure of. I bet they'll be nice, because I'm nice, and they'll be fun, too. One thing they won't have to worry about is having to live with lots of different families. I'll make sure of that."

BIBLIOGRAPHY

FOR CHILDREN:
Bunin, Sherry. *Is That Your Sister?* New York: Pantheon Books, 1976.
A true story about a transracially adopted black child in a Caucasian family. Black-and-white photographs in snapshot album format. Ages: 6–8.

Krementz, Jill. *How It Feels to Be Adopted.* New York: Knopf, 1982.
Nineteen children express their feelings about being adopted. Some have had reunions with their birth parents. Black-and-white photographs. Ages: 10 +

Powledge, Fred. *So You're Adopted.* New York: Scribners, 1982.
An adult adoptee describes what it's like to grow up adopted. Ages: 9 up.

Rosenberg, Maxine B. *Being Adopted.* New York: Lothrop, Lee & Shepard, 1984.
Three children explain how adoption affects their lives. Emphasis on transracial, transcultural adoption. Black-and-white photographs. Ages: 6–10.

———. *Making a New Home in America.* New York: Lothrop, Lee & Shepard, 1986.
The feelings and experiences of four children as they adjust

to their new life in the United States. Black-and-white photographs. Ages: 6–10.

Sobol, Harriet Langsam. *We Don't Look Like Our Mom and Dad.* New York: Coward-McCann, 1984.
Korean-born brothers describe how it feels to be transracially adopted. Black-and-white photographs. Ages: 6–9.

FOR ADULTS:
Du Prau, Jeanne. *Adoption.* New York: Julian Messner, 1981. Discusses feelings of adoptees at different ages. Section on adoptees' and their families' attitudes toward search.

Gilman, Lois. *The Adoption Resource Book.* New York: Harper & Row, 1984.
Describes ages and stages of adoptees as they adjust to their birth situation.

Henig, Robin Marantz. "Chosen and Given," *The New York Times,* September 11, 1988.
Discusses the pain adopted children carry for having been "given away" by their biological parents.

Jewett, Claudia L. *Adopting the Older Child.* Boston: The Harvard Common Press, 1978.
Focuses on the background of children adopted at ages five and older. Describes their patterns of behavior and adjustment problems as they become part of a new family.

———. *Helping Children Cope with Separation and Loss.* Boston: The Harvard Common Press, 1982.

Describes the mourning process adopted children experience and how adults can help the child get through grief.

Kaye, Kenneth. "Turning Two Identities Into One," *Psychology Today,* November 1988.
Encourages families to acknowledge the uniqueness of raising an adopted child while not maximizing the differences.

Margolies, Marjorie, and Ruth Gruber. *They Came to Stay.* New York: Coward, McCann & Geoghegan, 1976.
Personal account of a single parent's experience with her Korean- and Vietnamese-born daughters.

Melina, Lois Ruskai. *Raising Adopted Children.* New York: Harper & Row, 1986.
Provides concrete information on how parents can help their adopted children during different ages and stages of the child's life. Discusses special issues that older, transracial, or abused adoptees have to face.

———. *Making Sense of Adoption.* New York: Harper & Row, 1989.
Tells parents what children want to know about their adoption at various life stages and how to provide this information. Includes sample conversations, activities, and so on.

Plumez, Jacqueline Horner. *Successful Adoption.* New York: Harmony Books, 1982.
Overall view on what families experience when they adopt a young child. Appendix on agencies and organizations providing information on adoption.

Powledge, Fred. *The New Adoption Maze.* St. Louis: The C. V. Mosby Co., 1985.
Explains how adoption has changed over the years and what this means to the adoptee.

Sorosky, Arthur, and Annette Baran. *The Adoption Triangle.* New York: Anchor Press, 1978.
Describes the effects of court-sealed records on adoptees, birth parents, and adoptive parents. Criticizes adoption policies that foster fear and secrecy and offers a program to change attitudes concerning adoption.

SOURCES OF HELP

Adopted Child
P.O. Box 9362
Moscow, ID 83843
208-882-1181
A newsletter about life with adopted children, edited by Lois
Ruskai Melina.

Adoptive Families of America (formerly OURS, Inc.)
3307 Highway 100 N, Suite 203
Minneapolis, MN 55422
Parent support organization issuing newsletter on adoption
and selling merchandise relevant to adoptees. Chapters
throughout country.

Association for Children with Learning Disabilities
4156 Library Road
Pittsburgh, PA 15234
Referral organization for children and adults with learning
disabilities. Publishes a newsletter. Individual chapters
throughout the United States.

Child Help's
National Child Abuse Hotline USA
800-422-4453 (800-4-A-CHILD)

Child Welfare League of America
440 First Street, N.W., Suite 310
Washington, D.C. 20001
202-638-2952
Particularly concerned with children in temporary homes.
Extensive list of published books and journals.

National Association for Children of Alcoholics
31706 Coast Highway, Suite 201
South Laguna, CA 92677
Information and referrals for therapy and treatment programs for children of alcoholics; books and organizations;
local chapters; and support groups.

National Center for Children with Learning Disabilities
99 Park Avenue
New York, NY 10016
212-687-7211
Disseminates information for children with learning difficulties, e.g., about camps, schools.

National Committee for Adoption
1930 Seventeenth Street, N.W.
Washington, D.C. 20009-6207
202-328-1200
Issues *Adoption Factbook* and provides list of parent support
groups throughout country.

North American Council on Adoptable Children
1821 University Avenue, Suite 275
St. Paul, MN 55104

Lists current publications about adoption and offers resources and technical assistance for those involved with adoption.

PACER (Post Adoption Center for Education and Research)
447 Fifteenth Street, Room 200
Oakland, CA 94612
Provides information about adoption experience for adoptees and birth and adoptive parents.

Planned Parenthood
1-800-248-7797
Provides pregnancy option counseling, a program for pregnant adolescents, and reproductive health care, including birth control.

AFTERWORD

For a long time, adoptive parents and the profession-
als who work with adoptive families thought there were
two critical times in adopted children's lives: around the
age of six, when children first understand reproduction
well enough to understand adoption, and during ado-
lescence, when questions of identity normally arise. Typ-
ically, once parents answered their young children's
question, "Did I grow inside Mommy?", they breathed
a sigh of relief. The expectation was that adoption would
not be an issue again in their families until their children
became teenagers and perhaps indicated a desire to
meet their birth parents.

Now we know that the middle years of childhood are
also vitally important. (The middle childhood years are
usually considered to be the ages from seven to eleven,
but, of course, not all children mature at the same rate.)

103

As the children and adults in *Growing Up Adopted* make clear, this is a time of thoughtful questioning. But concerns and fears children have at this stage of their lives are not always shared with their parents.

Children younger than six tend to accept the idea of being adopted easily. However, school experiences and the mastery of new skills cause elementary school children to consider their adoption in a new light.

When they begin school, children discover the ways in which they differ from other children. Adopted children learn that most of their classmates live with at least one birth parent. Naturally, they become curious about the significance of this difference. Also, during the elementary school years, children work hard on developing information-gathering and problem-solving skills. Not surprisingly, they apply these skills to themselves—seeking to learn more about who they are, what their families are all about, and how they fit into the world.

The questions expressed by the children in this book are typical of adopted children in the middle childhood years:

"What do my birth parents look like?"

"Do I have any [biological] brothers or sisters?"

"Why didn't my birth parents keep me?"

Like Jamie, children in the middle years also wonder whether parents love a child born to them more than the one they've adopted. They wonder, too, whether adoption is permanent—can the birth parents reclaim them? for instance, or, as Joe believed, must they behave in a certain way to remain in their families?

Parents are sometimes surprised to hear that their children have questions like these because they have not verbalized such concerns. However, even parents who have discussed adoption openly from the beginning may find that during the middle years, troubling thoughts and fears may be hidden by a child's calm demeanor and apparent lack of interest in adoption. There are several explanations for this behavior.

First, as the narratives in *Growing Up Adopted* reveal, even when they are grown up, children sometimes think probing questions about their origins or an expressed desire to meet their birth parents will hurt their adoptive parents. Children may also keep their concerns to themselves because the answers they have been given in the past have not explained matters satisfactorily. Because of younger children's lack of sophistication about the world and the legal system, it is often difficult for them to fully comprehend a birth parent's situation and the permanency of adoption. Their ideas about why they were adopted may not fit with their parents' explanations, so their parents lose credibility.

Of course, as the conversations in *Growing Up Adopted* express so well, adoption is only one aspect of children's lives. At times it will have their full attention, while at other times sports, school, and friends will be foremost in their minds.

During the middle years, parents need to be alert to

subtle signs that their children are struggling with adoption issues. They can initiate conversations about adoption when it seems appropriate and natural. Most of all, they can encourage their children to feel free to express their thoughts—whether positive or negative—about being adopted. A large portion of my book *Making Sense of Adoption* gives specific suggestions for achieving good parent-child communication.

In the past, a book like *Growing Up Adopted* could not have been written. As Marsha describes, adoption has not always been discussed openly, even within the family. But there has been a growing awareness in recent years of the importance of helping children share their thoughts and feelings about adoption.

I would like to think that this openness will benefit those children who are adopted, particularly as they experience the questions and concerns typical of the middle childhood years. I would hope that opportunities for ongoing contact between adoptive and birth families will continue to be offered so that adopted children have an easier time getting their questions answered as they grow up. And I would hope that the encouragement being given adoptive parents today—through books, newsletters, and support groups—to understand and anticipate their children's issues will make their lives and their families' lives more emotionally secure.

It's important to remember that the recent changes in adoption philosophy and practice have not originated with psychologists or educators or social workers, but with adoptees themselves. Those who have had the courage to tell their stories have taught us much about what it is like to grow up adopted.

When we truly listen to the subjects in this book and to others who have been adopted, we can hear them saying that being curious about their birth parents in no way reflects a dissatisfaction with their adoptive parents; that honesty is essential in their lives; that adoption is an important part of them, but only one part of them; and that, like all of us, they wish they didn't have to suffer any losses.

By listening to adoptees, especially those who are still struggling, even as adults, to understand what adoption means, all of us who are adoptive parents or who work with adoptive families can be more sensitive to our children's needs.

Lois Ruskai Melina, author of *Raising Adopted Children* and *Making Sense of Adoption,* and editor and publisher, *Adopted Child* newsletter

INDEX